D1066328

Out There, Somewhere

John Morano

For Molly —
Now that you're in Skagway,
you're more 'Out There' than I
am!
5/05
Hope you enjoy
your visit to
SeaTopia...

John

Blue Works
🌍 **Port Orchard** 🌍 **Seattle** 🌍 **Tahuya** 🌍

Out There, Somewhere
copyright 2003 by John Morano
published by Blue Works

ISBN 1-59092-088-0
9 8 7 6 5 4 3 2
First edition January 2005

Cover and design by Buster Blue of Blue Artisan Designs.

For information about film, reprint or other subsidiary rights, please contact Mari Garcia at mgarcia@windstormcreative.com.

Blue Works is part of Windstorm Creative, a multi-division, international organization involved in publishing books in all genres, including electronic publications; producing games, toys, videos and audio cassettes as well as producing theatre, film and visual arts events. The wind with the gear center was designed by Buster Blue of Blue Artisan Designs and is a trademark of Blue Works.

Blue Works
c/o Windstorm Creative
Post Office Box 28
Port Orchard WA 98366
somewhere@windstormcreative.com
www.windstormcreative.com
360-769-7174 ph.fx

Blue Works is a member of Orchard Creative Group, Ltd.

Dedication

For Mom and Dad...

One of the most difficult feelings
I've ever had to express is my
gratitude, my amazement
for all that you've given
all that you've done
all that you've shown.

No one's ever had
better parents
than me...

Acknowledgments

My friends in SeaTopia and I would like to thank the following individuals for making this book possible:

As always, Kris for her patience and her love.

My two buddies, John and Vincent, for their never-ending enthusiasm, constant flow of creative thoughts and for being the kind of friends only sons can be.

Roger Rufe, for generously penning a wonderful introduction and for actually doing the things that I can only write about.

Jennifer and Cris DiMarco for believing in eco-literature, for patiently allowing me to deliver my manuscript 'slightly' after deadline, for making the publishing process enjoyable and for giving me a very special royalty, friendship.

Blue Works and Blue Artisan Designs for a thoughtful, attractive creation.

The Monmouth University community for a deep, continued support of my writing.

Samantha Weinberg for writing such a special book about coelacanths. *A Fish Caught in Time* is the perfect blend of science, journalism and history, wrapped in a wonderfully literate package. It helped me get to know Puta a little better.

Emley's Hill United Methodist Church. Now you know what I'm scribbling on the back of the bulletin during sermons.... You're always closer to God when you stand on the Hill.

Lastly, thank you God for giving me the words to tell stories about your creatures and their place in your world.

Introduction

The oceans cover 71 percent of our planet and they contain 97 percent of all living matter. Yet for most of the 6.3 billion people who live on land, ocean life remains largely out of sight and out of mind. But not to John Morano. In *Out There, Somewhere*, Morano brings that world alive for young adults and others by portraying a diverse community of creatures; from a rare coelacanth, to an injured sea turtle, to shrimp to dolphins to an intelligent octopus.

For 30 years, The Ocean Conservancy has worked to keep people mindful that the oceans are not another world, but are in fact a vital part of *our* world. Just as we depend upon them for food, oxygen, transportation, recreation, and climate control, the oceans depend upon us to protect them from the consequences of harmful human activities: overfishing, pollution, habitat destruction, and above all, from human apathy.

In *Out There, Somewhere*, Morano portrays the human tendency to view the oceans and ocean life as intended for human exploitation; in it, the main characters—including several fish, a sea turtle, a manatee, and some dolphins become showpieces in an aquarium. And just as there are all kinds of sea creatures in his novel, there are all kinds of people: poachers, fishers, aquarists torn between the need to make money and the desire to teach humans about ocean life, and scientists whose curiosity drives them to have a hand in exploiting marine species. Through all of this, Morano does something that few ocean writers do; he provides us with a unique perspective—that of the exploited animal. In so doing, he demonstrates just how profound and pervasive humans' effect on the oceans is. Entanglement, bycatch, and poaching all threaten the health of our oceans. And they all have a human origin. In *Out There, Somewhere*, we see how persistent these threats are. No ocean species in the book escapes the impacts of the "man-tide," as the ocean creatures refer to us humans. And that, I believe, is a fair portrayal of our influence.

This is science fiction, though not in the usual sense of the word. Although *Out There, Somewhere* is a novel, Morano has done his research, and he brings these creatures alive by looking at the details of their existence— the habitats they depend upon, the predators they fear, their unique social behaviors. And all these details serve to make them interesting and real to us, and to show us dimensions of ocean life that we rarely consider.

But this is much more than fiction describing the life that sea creatures lead in the shadow of human dominance. It's about the morality of human exploitation, the way we justify our actions under the guises of "economics" and "education." Is it, after all, better to bring ocean creatures to aquariums to educate people? Or should we allow them to remain in the habitats where they play critically important roles?

A manatee, Naillij, describes eloquently the problem that conservationists face—humans' prevailing attitude toward nature: "The man-tide ignores the balance. In fact, they violate it. Then they come in and try to make it right. They show themselves that they are more powerful than the spirit by destroying the balance. And then they fool themselves into thinking that by bringing things back to where they should have been all along, they have restored the balance, righted the wrong. But the wrong has still happened . . ."

Economic considerations continue to overshadow conservation and precaution. And this is shown in the character of Dave, the owner of the Sea-Topia aquarium, where many of the novel's characters end up on display. Although he is a thoughtful and principled conservationist, he is seduced by the possibility of economic gain and success: "The one commercial concession Dave had made, at the urging of the board, was to accept the coelacanth. The canth would be a fiscal home run, but like many profitable choices, Dave felt somewhat Faustian, like he had sold his soul to the devil . . . What Dave hoped was that the sheer educational value of the creature would somehow justify the personal betrayals." (92) Dave shows us how easily we can compromise our ethics when economic considerations enter the picture.

As it has for the past three decades, The Ocean Conservancy will continue to fight for effective laws that protect against human activities that threaten both healthy oceans and ocean life—habitat destruction, overfishing, entanglement, pollution, and trade in endangered species. We will continue to provide citizens with the means of speaking out on the oceans that we all share. And we will continue to educate the public about the world that lies largely hidden beneath the waves. We urge you to join us by visiting our website, www.oceanconservancy.org, and by learning how you can help to reverse the failing health of our oceans.

John Morano's eco-adventure series will undoubtedly help that cause by engaging young audiences and by dramatizing the interaction between people and ocean life.

Perhaps together we can change the prevailing human attitudes that have wreaked so much destruction in the past, and begin to build a new ocean ethic, whereby all people learn to appreciate all ocean life and become active ocean stewards, seeking to preserve healthy oceans for the benefit of present and future generations.

Roger T. Rufe, Jr.
President
The Ocean Conservancy

Out There, Somewhere

John Morano

Chapter One

Spare the Rod

Maputa sat quietly in her cave. The sun lingered high above the sea surrounding the Comoros Islands. She was not hiding. There was little Maputa feared in her world. Perhaps a Great White or some brazen rouge predator might try its luck, but the odds were against it. Her six foot long, three hundred pound grouper-like body was covered with such large serrated scales, almost armor plates in design, that few creatures would attempt an attack. Below her gentle eyes a wide mouth patched with short spiked teeth were both intimidating and functional.

When the setting sun moored beneath the surface of the sea, Maputa would emerge from her comfy cave, join friends and family, and begin the feeding that would last through the night. It was what she and her kind did everyday, what her kind had done for almost four hundred million years. If there ever was one, Maputa was a living fossil.

Although the man-tide believed Maputa and her kind had vanished with the dinosaurs at the end of the Cretaceous Period, some sixty-five million years ago, they had instead weathered every storm blown their way for millennia upon millennia. Since the dawn of the Devonian Epoch, four hundred and ten million years ago, the coelacanth has remained relatively unchanged. While mosasaurs, plesiosaurs and megalodons have given way to Great Whites, Giant Squid and the man-tide, Maputa and the other coelacanths continue on, virtually unfazed by the events of the world around them. But that was about to change.

Maputa was proud of her cobalt blue color. White scale-flecks matched the white sponges and oyster shells gathered around the face of the cave. Like most coelacanths, Maputa felt comfortable living below deep reefs and steep volcanic slopes in water anywhere from three hundred to two thousand or more feet deep. The cool dark currents calmed the ancient fish, assuring her that all was well. She was beneath it all.

The canth liked to hover and drift in the current. Her excellent night vision and unique fins, each situated on its own short wrist, allowed her to feed opportunistically as candidates crossed her hungry path. Devoted disciples of the spirit-fish, Maputa and her group would often interrupt their feeding, bow their heads in unison and give thanks... for the evening, for their lives.

Maputa was hungrier than she normally would have been, probably because of the pups she had carried within her for almost a year. The expectant mother was well aware of her condition; she could actually give birth at any time. This thought made her anxious. She worried her pups might be born so far from her cave that they would become instant prey. But in the deep water, with her family all around her, Maputa opted for nourishment over safety, a choice mothers of all species grappled with.

The sheaf of canths, the term for a group that included several families, was carried into more open water. In unison they bowed their heads, raised their unique three-pronged caudal fins and hung motionless in the silence, waiting to detect movement or the soft electrical pulse of life in their sensitive rostral organs. Then they would feed. The canths were hunting for something else, as well. It was at these moments, together, feeding, that they most often heard the voice of Seaqoyit. They listened and they spoke.

Maputa was doing what her ancestors had done for over four thousand centuries, long before there was an Atlantic or a Pacific ocean, when Morocco and New Jersey were neighbors. The canths had found a harmony, a place, a way. Her family had lived on this spot for more than a million years. Those in her shock, a collection of sheaves, rarely ranged more than a few miles from their roosting caves. They only ventured beyond when all the caves were filled. These days, however, there were more canths returning than leaving.

As they completed their first meditation of the evening, they waved their tribolated tail fins in unison and raised their heads. Maputa's brother swam up beside her. He had a glow in his eyes that spilled out over his blue scales. Mombassa knew his sister would give birth soon, that she would add to the life of the sheaf and the diversity of the sea.

"Puta, how do you feel?" he whispered.

"Good enough to eat, but I think I will feed quickly tonight and return early."

"Could they come tonight?" Mombassa asked. "Should we go back *now*?"

Maputa half smiled, "It could happen... probably not, but the pups could come. Either way, I still have to eat. Do something for me..."

"Anything," the large male replied.

"I'll keep working this spot, but if any of the others happen upon an easy feed, will you come and get me? I'd like to get this done quickly."

"I'll spread the word." Mombassa swam off to pass along his sister's request. The others would surely cooperate. What was good for Maputa was good for them as well. One thing the canths had learned over time was that, generally speaking, cooperation was healthier than competition.

Maputa began searching for her own meal. Snapping up a squid here and a cuttlefish there, she rose to a depth much higher than she would usually work, and she stumbled upon something very intriguing. It sat motionless on the terrace of a volcanic ridge in only two hundred feet of water. Difficult for the coelacanth to describe, more so to fully understand, what she saw was a rigid rectangular net. The mesh of the large net was hard, but so thin it seemed delicate. Maputa's pressure-sensitive lateral line and her keen eyesight picked up fish swimming inside the mesh. The net was full of fish. A few were dead, but most were darting back and forth, unable to escape. For some reason, they could not find the large hole that seemed obvious to Maputa.

She rubbed up against the container, the electroreceptors in her snout were buzzing as they picked up the frenetic blasts of life passing through the water. If she could enter the container, she could eat her fill and return to her cave. Then if she gave birth, she would not have to leave her babies for many days. This was just what she needed. But Maputa was not so dazzled by the sight of such a succulent smorgasbord that she would neglect to consider her escape. If this thing could contain all these fish, it might also be capable of entrapping her. The crafty canth studied the contraption and the fish inside. She reasoned that they were so panicked they had trapped themselves. If she could keep her cool inside the mesh, she could get out as easily as she got in. If that failed, she was so large and so powerful, the canth was convinced she could smash or chew her way through the diminutive mesh.

Maputa sniffed the fish inside. The catch smelled good, but the mesh also bore the trace of a strange scent, something the sea had not completely washed away, something it could not wash away. Maputa, however, saw only the temptation of the incredible feast. She laid her side against the mesh. It dented easily beneath her bulk. The canth located the opening, flattened her fins, contracted her girth and wriggled forward. The tunnel that guided her into the rectangle opened into a more spacious chasm predominately filled with lantern fish, Maputa's favorite food.

She sucked them in, two and three at a time, swallowing both live and dead. A dust cloud rose as the mesh ripped at the sediment it sat upon. Soon the lantern fish were consumed. Maputa felt lucky that she could eat so much, so easily. It was not feeding the way the spirit had intended, but it was the most blissful banquet of her life. She satisfied herself thinking about the nourishment her pups would get in this vital late stage of their development. It was time to go home.

The canth turned back to the tunnel that had carried her to the lantern fish. She had some difficulty shifting her body within the container, but in the end managed to turn herself around. Maputa peered into the hole. It seemed smaller going out than it was coming in, which was somewhat true since she now faced the smaller end of the funnel-shaped tunnel. But Maputa reasoned that if the hole allowed her to enter, it would certainly allow her to exit. Its size was a constant. She swam into the opening.

The same funnel that enabled her fins and scales to fold down and helped her slide easily as she entered, now caught her fins and ripped at her scales with its exposed tight end. It grabbed her and held her inside, preventing the coelacanth from getting through the opening. Maputa withdrew and considered her dilemma. Apparently, she could not fit into the same hole that carried her in. She would have to find another way out. Scanning the mesh for a weak spot that she could work open, Maputa heard a scratchy, squeaky voice say, "That's what you get for being greedy." The canth felt the minute electric charge tickle her snout and located the source of the voice instantly. She could see exactly where it came from, but could not quite identify the creature. Then, as he shifted his position, Maputa saw him clearly.

A shrimp, almost transparent, looked up at the huge fish and smiled. "If it looks too good to be true, it usually is," he said.

"Thanks for the advice," Maputa replied. "It's especially helpful telling me that *after* I'm stuck in here."

"Well, you didn't consult me *before* you entered."

"I'm not consulting me now, either, but you're still passing out information, aren't you?"

"Good point," the shrimp conceded. He could afford to be amused by the coelacanth's predicament, since he was small enough to come and go as he pleased.

"Know a way out of here?" Maputa asked.

The shrimp scanned the container, moved its eyestalks in a variety of directions, nodded its little head and said, "Nope."

Maputa resumed her search. She examined every corner of the container, nudging it, testing it with her head. While the mesh had some give to it, it did not break or tear. A little more desperate, Maputa threw her bulk at the mesh, hoping to create a crack or hole. The rectangle rolled off the cliff. It tumbled down the bank of the dormant volcano. Rocks and debris were jarred loose. A small avalanche rained down on the container when it finally settled on another outcropping. Dented and twisted, the mesh held. Its give, which Maputa assumed made it weaker, had actually made it stronger. The container did not defy stress, it absorbed it. Still, Maputa gathered herself for another try. She suddenly felt strange, a pain that was not exactly painful. Perhaps she had injured herself in the canth-alanche. Then she saw what had happened and understood the peculiar sensation.

Swimming next to her, inside the container, was a tiny blue fish. Peaceful, beautiful, innocent. It was her child — her first-born. The puzzling pleasant pain returned. The pup was joined by another... and another... and another. In moments, seven small pups were nuzzling their mother. Maputa drew them closer with her fins, felt the life within them, thanked the spirit-fish and prepared for the journey to her cave, their cave. Nilmah, her mate, would be so happy. And then the world returned.

Sitting on the dorsal fin of one of the youngsters, the shrimp dusted himself off. He looked seriously at Maputa and said, "Would you mind notifying me the next time you decide to throw me down a steep ledge? I might want to prepare myself... or leave."

Maputa ignored the shrimp. She had no time for distractions and no interest in anything other than escaping with her young. That same interest, however, she was galvanized by what happened next. One of the pups was waving at her from the other side of the mesh. It was close to her, but it was definitely outside the container. The fully formed little canth, who looked remarkably like his father, paddled over to the banged-up tunnel and started to enter the container once again.

"STOP!" Maputa screamed. "Don't move another fin." The little one froze.

Maputa was faced with a real problem. Was her child safer inside the container, next to her, shielded from predators, or better off outside where it would be free to flee, but alone? The new mother felt a surge against her lateral line; something large approached. "Incoming... Get inside little one," she whispered to the precocious pup. Maputa hid her babies beneath her and prepared to fend off whatever came through the twisted tunnel.

Out of the dusty dark below the ledge rose the intruder. Mombassa shook his head. He looked worried. "What have you done?"

"There is no free lunch," his sister lamented.

"You can say that again. Let's get you out of here."

"I'm not sure it's going to be so easy. And I have another surprise for you." Maputa leaned to one side and her children swam out to meet their uncle.

"You're just full of surprises, aren't you?" Mombassa smiled.

Maputa gestured to the pups and said, "I *was* full of surprises."

"They're incredible," the proud uncle gushed, as one emerged from the container and touched Mombassa.

"Let's try this," Maputa suggested, "you take them back to the caves. Have Gunung look after them. Then come right back here with Nilmah and see if you can get me out of here."

"I don't know..."

"There's no choice. And it'll all go better if we know the pups are safe. Don't worry about me. I'm not going anywhere."

Mombassa nodded, gathered the pups and swam off, hoping not to encounter a feeding tiger shark along the way.

Alone in the mesh, feeling slightly claustrophobic, the young mother watched her children swim down into the deep. She hoped that Mombassa and Nilmah would return quickly. Once more, the coelacanth tried to push herself through the twisted tunnel. Once again, she could not fit.

"I have good news... and I have bad news," Maputa heard. It was that same scratchy, squeaky voice from before.

The transparent shrimp danced defiantly through the small holes in the mesh, teasing the canth. He repeated, "Good news and bad news, my friend."

"Just gimme the good news."

"Sorry. It's not one or the other. It's all or nothing. What'll it be?"

"Surprise me," Maputa mumbled.

"Well, here's the good news. I've seen these before. It's something made by the man-tide to catch fish. Looks like this one works pretty well."

"That's the good news? Once again, you give great info when it's totally useless!"

"But I'm not done yet. The good news is that these things usually have a long tentacle that reaches all the way to the surface. The man-tide returns on a floating island and pulls this up. Whatever happens next to the fish, I really can't say."

The canth stared at the shrimp. "I'm still waiting for the *good* news."

"This one has no tentacle..."

"So?"

"So, you can't be pulled up to the floating island. They can't get you. Believe me, that's good news."

"That," Maputa nodded, "is kind of good." She thought about her situation and felt some relief that it was probably just a matter of time before Nilmah and Mombassa freed her from the container. Her growing grin, however, disappeared as she asked, "What's the bad news?"

"The bad news is, there's no tentacle on this and they won't be able to pull you up."

Confused, Maputa countered, "But you said that was the good news?"

"Ah," the shrimp smiled, "like most things, it's how you look at it." His left eye looked left, while his right eye looked right. Then the left eye looked up, while the right eye looked down to illustrate the assertion. "It is good that the man-tide can't remove you, but it is also bad. How will you ever get out of here?"

"When Nilmah and Mombassa return, they'll get me out."

"I hope you're right, my friend."

The shrimp and the coelacanth waited. They continued to explore the mesh for a crack or an opening. Maputa began to breathe more deeply. Her heart began to beat harder. She was scared. She had a feeling that her life was about to change: A very unsettling feeling for any coelacanth. The timeless tranquility of her existence had been interrupted by this container and she was left with no control over her fate. But before full blown panic replaced her fear, Mombassa returned with Nilmah.

The two canths swam in hard, their underwater surge washing over Maputa and sending the shrimp spiraling in their wake.

"Tell me my pups are safe!"

"Our children are safe," Nilmah answered. "Now, let's get you out of here. The last thing in the sea I need is to have to drag you back to the caves like this. I'll wind up with my mate spending the rest of her life in a container."

"You can forget about having anymore pups," Mombassa teased.

The humor of the two males eased the tension. Maputa became less anxious, but it was merely the calm before the storm. A bump, a soft thud nudged the top of the mesh. Nimah became quiet. He looked to Mombassa. They both looked up as another thud struck the mesh.

"It has begun," Mombassa mouthed.

"Yes, it is night," Nilmah added.

The man-tide had arrived, lowering their bait into the sea. It was very rare that a coelacanth would actually approach the bait. It was not really intended for them. Occasionally, a starving, stupid specimen might attempt a lazy meal, but even the dimmest coelacanth understood the danger of a fish hanging from a tentacle. Bait was resting on the top of the very mesh that held Maputa.

Gesturing upward, the female said, "This can't be good."

"The first thing we have to do," Mombassa declared, "is take you down."

Nilmah pushed the mesh against his face and whispered to his mate, "Yes, you'll be safer in the deep water… and perhaps this mesh will weaken as we drag you down. Are you ready, Maputa?"

She nodded and prepared herself for the prolonged tumble down the face of the dormant volcano.

"Let's go!" Mombassa called.

The two large males pushed the mesh forward. Maputa kept herself afloat, swimming along with her mate and her brother so there would be less resistance. The container slid along the ridge, dislodging barnacles, sponges and other growth. As it reached the edge of the ledge, Maputa sucked in a deep breath, sealed her gill covers and prayed that the spirit fish would release her. The canths tried to lift the container as they pushed forward, but it was too heavy.

Nilmah whispered, "Don't worry, the mesh will never hold up. We'll meet you at the bottom."

They shoved it over, hundreds of feet of water beneath it with occasional coral and rock jutting out from the face of the volcano, waiting to rip the mesh open and release Maputa, but something strange happened. Although the mesh was pushed clear of the ledge, it did not sink. It hung for a moment in the open water, hovering. The container defied gravity.

"It is the spirit," Mombassa declared. "My sister is saved."

Then the mesh and Maputa began to slowly rise. All at once, the three canths understood what was happening. As they had pushed the container along the ledge, the bait dropped by the man-tide became locked onto the mesh. That is why Maputa did not drop to the bottom. The tentacles from the floating islands held the mesh. And now it was being pulled to the surface.

Nilmah swam above the mesh and tore at a line. Mombassa followed his lead. Maputa bit at the bait that dangled from the mesh, ignoring the hooks that she knew were hidden inside. Powerful jaws and sharp spiked teeth were usually more than a match for anything the sea might throw at them, as they had proven over time, but this mesh, these tentacles tearing Maputa from her home, were not of the sea. This was the creation of the man-tide. Why were they here? What were they doing?

One of the tentacles snapped. The container lurched and Maputa tumbled against the side. Nilmah and Mombassa each worked on one of the two remaining tentacles. The closer they came to the surface, the warmer the water became. They could feel the change in pressure. The canths were uncomfortable, dizzy, but they continued their struggle. The lights from the floating islands that danced and winked from above became larger, brighter, blinding. Time, something the canths had always had so much of, was running out.

Smitty was in his early seventies, a retired telephone line technician from Long Island now living on the northeast coast of Florida. He told people that it was a law in New York that once you turned seventy you either had to retire and move to Florida, or go to jail. Lean and strong, with thick bristly white hair, he was so calm and understated that whenever he said something funny it took a moment for his listener to get the joke. For a moment, everyone always believed whatever he said. He could say there were three green suns in the sky and before his claim was dismissed, he knew you'd check the sky just to make sure. The only clue that he might be joking was the hint of a smile that always seemed to grace his weathered face.

Smitty was an honest, happy guy and always had been. The idea that the grass was greener someplace else never meant anything to him. He had all he ever needed in his wife Belle, their three children and his grandkids. Smitty knew there was nothing more than that, not really, except for an occasional slice of homemade chocolate cake.

And even though he was retired, he couldn't stop working. He just worked for free now. Driving home along the road that ran down the coast, something caught his eye on the side of the road, so he drifted onto the shoulder and parked. Smitty watched a pair of black-backed gulls peck at something on a dune. Several other birds circled, waiting for their turn. Smitty knew that there were endangered gopher tortoises in the area and wondered if a nest of eggs was being plundered. He climbed out of the cab and crossed the road. He approached the dune quietly. The birds would scatter whether he waved his arms and shouted or not.

As he got closer, he could see the shell. There was movement. It was alive. Pleased, Smitty said quietly, "You may not think so, but today is your lucky day." He climbed the dune, violating the "No Trespassing" ordinance posted on a sign.

When he reached down to rescue the sand-covered crawler, Smitty was surprised. It was not a gopher tortoise at all. With both hands, he picked up a half-dead, half-grown sea turtle. Too young to be laying eggs and much too large to be a hatchling, Smitty didn't know what to make of it. The adolescent had a crack in its shell and a length of fishing line twisted tightly into the infected flesh of a rear flipper. The flipper looked like an old injury, while the crack in the shell seemed recent. Smitty guessed that the flipper impeded his mobility and awareness so much that a boat must have run it over, cracking the shell.

"Yes, indeed, it sure is your lucky day," Smitty repeated. He carried the turtle back to his truck, laid him as best he could in a cooler, poured in a few buckets of fresh seawater, turned the pick-up around and drove back to where he had been working all day, where he knew the animal could be cared for.

Norton, a stargazer, sat with his compact muscular body buried deep in the sand. His eyes, which were mounted on the very top of his head, could see above the sand and had almost three hundred sixty degrees of visibility when unobstructed on the flats. He could spot whatever approached or left the reef without being spotted himself. He was called a stargazer because his eyes naturally gazed up to the stars. Just under Norton's pronounced peepers was a huge mouth. With a body shaped like a funnel, the wide end being a massive oral cavity, the short, squat swallowing pot could erupt from the sand, jaws agape, and engulf his meal. Although he didn't look it, Norton was extremely quick. He also carried an impressive electrical charge, should something drop down on him.

Another virtue he possessed grew out of necessity. Since he wasn't really fast enough to chase his meals down, he needed to be patient, and he was. Stargazers understood that when a meal wandered by they would usually get only one shot at it, so they waited and waited until the prey was literally on top of them.

It was a slow feeding day, even by Norton's standards, but he was pleased with his placement, so he dug in deeper... and waited. If Norton was anything, he was a profishional. He saw movement, a flash on the flats and a sandy cloud rising.

Come to Norton, he thought.

Some type of wounded fish or coral worm was struggling against the tug of the tide. The stargazer liked that. It meant that the prey might be tired when it finally reached him. It would be a quick and easy end.

It was almost impossible to be a stargazer and not feel the spirit. Spending days gazing at the clouds above the sea and nights gazing at the stars, Norton had developed a solid understanding of the way of the spirit-fish, and while many were much better at it than him, the gazer was proud that he had become a fishtian.

Although he was relieved and satisfied when he ate, Norton took no joy in causing another's demise. He believed that there was no room in the ocean for cruelty or malice. His pride of predation was always tempered by the fact that a life was taken. And every time he thanked Seaqoyit for nourishment, he also asked for forgiveness.

Norton saw the long white strip waving and struggling. It inched closer. Only something injured or ill would draw so much attention to itself, he thought. The only other creatures to be so bold were the ones who didn't care if they were noticed, because nothing would dare eat them, like the nudibranch. This, however, was obviously no nudibranch.

In the back of his mind, Norton was concerned that some other fish might spot his meal and devour it before it reached him. He toyed with the idea of emerging from the sand and trying to chase it down, since the prey didn't look like it could out-swim him, but in the end, Norton stayed where he was. The gazer recalled a saying his father recited when he was teaching his son to hunt. "Always dance with the fish that brung ya." Norton would do just that. He knew how to play to his strengths.

The white worm-like creature drew nearer. It approached in short hops, would rest a few seconds, allow the silt to settle, hop a little further and rest a little more... all the while, heading directly at Norton. It had no idea he was waiting.

When the sand surrounding his hiding spot began to move, Norton struck. He burst from below, mouth wide open and swallowed the meal in a milli-second. Before a barracuda could blink, the white strip of meat was buried inside the belly of the beast. Initially, there was no struggle. This pleased Norton. "No strain, no pain," he mumbled to himself. And then the pain arrived.

Norton felt a sharp rip, a searing slash below his ribs. Some kind of dorsal spine, he thought, had been thrust into the lining of his stomach. The stargazer instinctively tried to eject its meal, regurgitating as forcefully as he could. A second later, Norton saw the thin white strip float past his face, but the pain inside him only got worse. A lone Bonita raced by, swallowed the strip and continued on its way, smooth silver scales sparkling in the sun. Norton felt an excruciating tug. He was being dragged across the sand, pulled from the sea, ripped from his home.

Ignoring the pain, fighting for his life, the fish tried to swim in the opposite direction. Struggling and rolling along the sand, he saw it... a single long, thin tentacle. It stretched as far as he could see. He felt it against his body. It slid under his scales, got tangled in his fins. Norton bit at the line, but could not sever it. The stargazer knew what waited at the other end, at the end of the line. It was the man-tide. It was his death. Norton needed a new strategy.

On the surface of the sea the fisherman felt the tug. He watched with pleasure as the tip of his rod bent down, almost pointing to the fish below. The drag whined its warning that a "keeper" was taking line. Bao tightened the drag and began to reel, wondering to himself what was on the other end. He could usually tell by the way the fish fought what he had hooked, but it was still too early to answer that question.

When Norton felt a little slack in the tentacle, he thought he could escape. He shook his body in violent spasms, but the hook held. Once again the gazer was dragged back toward the man-tide's floating island. He could see it perched on the water. Since he felt that he could not out-tug the tentacle, he would try another move. Norton shot directly at the floating island as fast as he could swim. He hoped to pass under it and take refuge in the dense hammer coral just beyond. With luck, the razor sharp coral might cut the tentacle or tangle it so that he could not be pulled.

Norton threw everything he had into the dash. Exhausted, but undaunted, he passed directly under the blue bottom of the island. Although it was still attached, the tentacle hung loose in the sea. Norton saw the coral clearly and prepared to dive into it, twisting and tangling the line as much as possible.

Bao cranked his reel furiously, trying to take up the slack that the fish had created. Nothing good could come of a limp line. The fisherman found that out when he saw the small tangled nest on the spool of his spinning reel. Hoping not to lose the fish, Bao pulled on a fillet mit, dropped the rod and pulled the line with his hands. He'd worry about the tangle later.

Norton had a little more on the line, literally, than Bao. And he too was determined to win. When his coral oasis was just a few fins away, he felt as if he had triumphed. The stargazer struggled harder. He felt the first sharp scrape of the stone coral against his ventral fins. A coral cut never felt so good. Norton prayed to the spirit-fish that he'd have the chance to visit the cleaning station and have his cut looked after.

While his prayers were undoubtedly heard, the answer was not encouraging. Norton was suddenly bumped from below. Something tore at his anal fin. Another attack came from above. A pack of jacks cruising the inner banks of Makoona found the weary gazer hanging on a hook too appetizing. Four or five youngsters began their attack. Had they been a little larger, a little hungrier, they would have made fast work of Norton. Feeling no urgency, they raced in randomly to gnaw at the tangled fish, who tried his best to dodge their rushes while he was being dragged away from the coral, back to the floating island.

Norton knew it was over. The vibrant colors of life that decorated his scales faded to a dull grey. Barely alive, feeling as though he had begun to leave his body behind, Norton wondered where he would die: Would it be in the sea with the juvenile jacks, or out of the water with the man-tide? If he had to die, if the time was now, Norton decided to die like a fish, to feed the balance that he was part of his entire life. The stargazer fought the line, not so he could escape the hook, but so that he could escape the horrible end that came to fish who left the sea. The longer he stayed in the water, the longer the jacks had to end his life with dignity. And so, Norton fought with all he had left for the right to return his life to the sea that had always nourished him.

When Bao finally boated his catch, he was tempted to toss the beaten-up fish back, but an impulse like that rarely moved the opportunistic fisherman. Looking more closely, he was surprised by what had emerged from the water. It was one of the few times in his fishing life that he not only couldn't tell what was on the line by the way it fought, but he couldn't tell what was on the line when he held it in his hands, either. It was a fish he had never seen before. Immediately, Bao appreciated its rarity. While some would have gently returned it, due to its uniqueness, Bao dropped it into a red cooler and poured in some fresh sea water. To him, rarity meant value. Not to the diversity of the sea, but to the Filipino broker who would buy the fish. If it survived.

The cooler was large, so Bao had created four compartments by dropping a chicken wire insert into the box. The individual cells were reserved for special catches. Bao hoped the fish would perk up before he came ashore. A healthy fish always sold better.

The fish hit the water in the cooler and rolled onto its side. Bao watched it and noticed something else that suggested value. A small red tag hung loosely from one of its frayed fins. Bao tore it free and tossed the tag overboard. It could only complicate what he hoped would be an easy sale. Whether the battered creature wound up in someone's fish tank, on a plate smothered in scampi, in a mason jar or some other place mattered not to Bao, as long as a few dollars wound up in his pocket. This was his religion.

Norton really had no idea what was happening to him. He had been taken from the water of Makoona only once before. The man-tide hung a thick red hair on him and let him go, only after Norton delivered every fish-o-watt he could muster into his captor. At the moment, he was drained from the ordeal and unsure of what to expect next. In fact, the frightened fish wasn't completely sure that he was still alive. The bright whiteness that surrounded the clear water in the cooler, combined with the sunlight streaming in, made Norton think that he had surely begun his journey to the spirit-fish. He was calmed by the thought that he had escaped before the man-tide could use his flesh. He looked forward to meeting his maker, the one who had created the glorious coral reef that was Norton's home. For a fish who spent most of his life gazing into the heavens, this was an incredible moment.

Norton heard the words as they spilled into the blinding whiteness of the cooler. *The spirit is calling,* he thought.

"Wow, what happened to you?"

Puzzled (surely the creator would know the answer to his own question), Norton answered, "Did you not see? I was taken."

"I really can't see much from in here. But it looks like you put up quite a fight."

"How could you not see?" Norton pressed. "You are the spirit, the giver and taker of life. There is nothing you don't see."

Little bubbles trickled through the water, sparkling as they floated and popped. It was laughter. "You think I'm the spirit? Ha! You musta been in a fight. I'm not the spirit and you're not on your way to meet the creator. We're just two fish out of water, my friend."

"You're not the spirit-fish?"

"Shell, no…"

Suddenly Bao placed a wire insert over the walls of the cooler to keep the catch from jumping, climbing or spilling out. Then he snapped on a flimsy lid with one end propped open so air could circulate. It kept the sun from overheating the water.

Ignoring the instant darkness, Norton said, "Tell me something good. At this point, I'll take whatever you got."

The voice replied, "You're alive."

"That's all you got? How about where we are going? Or who you are? Or what you are?"

"I can't tell you where we're going, but I can tell you who I am. I'm Cariam."

"The octopus? The son of Binti and Molo?"

"That's me."

"I knew them! Well, I may not be speaking with the spirit-fish, but I think you're about the next best thing."

"I don't know," the octopus said, surveying their situation, "I think my parents were a little better at reaching Seaqoyit than I am. Just look at this mess…."

The large shiny car sped up to the curb, deposited a passenger and then raced away, the driver never realizing she had left the most precious part of her life behind on the curb. There were a lot of things the driver didn't realize. Her beauty would fade, her fancy car would be traded in, the man she raced to meet would not be what she hoped for, and the youngster she pushed aside would be connected to her forever. Many of these things she never would realize, of course, until it was too late.

Samantha walked toward the entrance to the aquarium while digging through her bookbag, an old retro *Flipper* number that someone her age, if she had any sense of style, would have replaced years ago. It was, after all, 1978. But Samantha wasn't concerned with things like that. In fact, most people thought she wasn't concerned with anything at all.

Why the girl fumbled for the crumbled season pass puzzled the woman at the ticket booth. The ticket-taker could set her watch to Samantha's arrival. The girl showed up everyday at 3:14 and stayed until closing. Ever since Samantha's mom realized that a season pass to SeaTopia was cheaper than a baby-sitter or an after school program, SeaTopia became Samantha's second home. Lately, it was more like her first home. The fourteen-year-old didn't complain. It wasn't in her nature. But there was another reason Samantha didn't complain. She didn't speak. She was capable, but generally chose not to. Occasionally, she flashed a shallow grin, rarely a frown, and although there were tears, others were not permitted to see them. The less noise she made, the less emotional she was, the less Samantha was noticed, which was fine with her.

And just because she didn't speak, didn't mean that Samantha wasn't intelligent. Her grades in junior high were good, though not nearly as good as she could make them. But if she ever did her best work, she might be noticed. Samantha never asked questions, wrote opinions or expressed a personal view, not in school, not anywhere.

One of the reasons SeaTopia suited Samantha so well was that she could remain invisible. Other than the staff who worked there, who would notice her? All the people who visited came for the day and most never returned. Samantha had been asked many times, "Where you from, young lady?" No one realized that in some ways she was as much from SeaTopia as the fish in the tanks. At the aquarium, she was just another face in the crowd, just another teen-ager staring into the tanks.

Samantha began her visit with the daily trek to the concession stand, otherwise known as The Conch Shack. She was, to her dismay, a familiar face to the concession stand workers. Samantha's mother usually gave her daughter five dollars for a "treat," which was actually dinner. Millie, the cashier, smiled, raised three fingers and the chef gathered together a number three special. The girl handed over her money, picked up the food with one hand and her change with the other. She walked quietly across the courtyard and settled at her favorite table. Eating early enabled her to beat the crowd and get good seating. She liked to sit in the most remote corner of the courtyard. The privacy was nice, but the view was better. The table looked out onto the beach just beyond the aquarium. Samantha liked to breathe the salty wet air and listen to the waves collapsing on the hard sand.

After the last chicken nugget was gone, Samantha sipped her soda and began her homework. She liked to get it out of the way before she looked in on her friends in the tanks.

Nilmah and Mombassa could not cut the remaining tentacle. When a corner of the tank breached the surface, one of the man-tide reached into the water and grasped the catch. Soon two others gaffed the mesh and hauled it from the sea. Maputa pressed her face into the lowest corner, crying to Nilmah and Mombassa, "My babies... Tell them I'm sorry..." And then Maputa was gone, dragged from the sea, ripped from her world. The coelacanth, blinded by the bright lights of the boats, glimpsed the eyes of the man-tide and fell into unconsciousness. It was over.

Her mate and her brother swam deeper into the sea. They stayed directly under the floating island, praying for a miracle.

Although they were fishing for lantern fish, they knew exactly what was lying on the deck. It was a protected, endangered species older than the islands, older than the caves. They were not allowed to keep these fish. As a matter of fact, the longest any one of these creatures survived in the hands of man was no more than several days. Usually, they wouldn't even survive the trip to shore. Many speculated that the sudden change in pressure from the deep water where they lived as they rose to the surface accounted for their demise. Others believed it was the rapid change in temperature. Some speculated that the change in oxygen content or the stress of being captured and transported was the cause. Perhaps all of these things, and more.

The boats gathered. The old salts looked the fish over. It was decided that Maputa had perished in the trap. "Incidental kill." As if those two words should ever be placed next to each other, an oxymoron if ever there was one. Many times, while fishing for one species, others would fall prey to the nets and traps that weren't really intended for them. And while it was illegal to capture a live coelacanth, one could bring in a carcass. If it was well-preserved, a museum or a university would certainly pay good money for the fish. The two fishermen could not load the fish onto their galawa, a canoe-like vessel with double outriggers, not much different than the original craft used by the island's Indonesian settlers during the first century. So they slipped a stringer into its mouth and through its gills to drag the canth to shore.

Once the outside world became aware that a coelacanth population existed off the coast of the Comoros, interested professionals began to gather, all hoping to see, or perhaps capture, one of the incredible creatures. But when an international moratorium was adopted and it became clear that no one would be taking a coelacanth home, most scientists lost interest. Prior to the legislation, a group interested in protecting coelacanths constructed a shelter to humanely house one or two specimens while they awaited transport. The facility featured a tank that contained cooled, pressurized ocean water, dimly lit to replicate the fish's natural setting. A small grotto was even constructed out of cement so the fish could take cover, easing its stress.

After the moratorium, the environmental group turned its attention to methods of releasing accidentally hooked coelacanths. They came up with an ingenious inverted hook system which prevented quite a few canths from becoming incidental kill. The shelter fell into a state of disrepair, and the locals plundered the facility, walking off with cinderblocks, PVC and other useful hardware.

When the fishermen returned to shore, they went directly to the abandoned shelter, tightened a few couplings, replaced a gasket, turned on a generator and fired up the pumps. Even with two of the building's walls virtually gone, the tank collected cold water. The large canth was dumped into the pool. She drifted in the current created by the pumps, rolling and turning at the mercy of the flow until she was pinned between the wall of the tank and the face of the grotto that jutted out into the water.

Before they left, two of the local fishermen dropped large carcasses of more common commercial fish into the tank. One quipped, "As long as we're keeping that dinosaur fresh, I might as well have my catch cooled."

His colleague replied, "Yeah, we'll clean them later."

Smitty drove past the parking lot and the main entrance. He swung around behind the facility and stepped through a private staff entrance.

"Haven't you left yet?" a custodian called out.

"Sure did. Now I'm back. You seen Dave around?"

"I think he's over with the manatee in rehab."

Smitty found Dave, SeaTopia's head aquarist, on his way to one of the large outdoor tanks carrying a long length of PVC.

"Hey Smitty, glad you haven't left yet. Check this out. We're gonna run two of these pipes on the bottom of the tank, pump air through them and see if the rising bubbles will keep the fish separated. Think it'll work?"

"Don't see why it wouldn't." Smitty looked the PVC over

and added, "If the holes were a little smaller, you'd get a tighter wall of bubbles."

"Hey, good thought." Dave handed the pipe to Smitty. "Why don't you see what you can do with this?"

"Sure, but there's no free lunch, you know. I've got something I want you to take a look at."

Dave followed Smitty to the pick-up. He saw the injured turtle in the cooler and carefully examined it.

"Can you help it?" Smitty asked.

"You know I can... but endangered species mean more paperwork..."

"Don't worry, I'll do the paperwork. You just sign it."

Dave smiled.

"And, I'll make you the greatest wall of bubbles you've ever seen."

Dave nodded, "Fair enough." He returned his attention to the turtle.

Carrying the creature to the rehab center at SeaTopia, Dave frowned and said, "I think he'll lose this rear flipper." He grimaced as if it was his own limb that was bound by fishing line, oozing and festering. In a way it was Dave's limb. He was one of those people who didn't dwell on differences. He saw connections. His empathy didn't end with humans. Inalienable rights, compassion was extended to anything alive. And that's why Smitty had taken the turtle to Dave.

Chapter Two
Everybody into the Pool!

After filling the turtle with potent antibiotics, Dave set him up in a large tank connected in a figure eight to a second tank where a mature manatee munched heads of lettuce. The manatee lumbered over to the rope fence that separated the tanks, rose to the surface and laid her head across the taught top line. Leafy greens spilled from her jowls. "How are you doing? Want some lettuce?"

The turtle, a little dazed and confused, replied, "Not very hungry right now." Seeing the net and the tank, he asked, "How do I get out of here?"

The manatee giggled, "You don't want to get out. They'll take good care of you here."

The turtle noticed his neighbor's back. There were raw scars running deep across her shoulders. Then he saw the flipper. Her rear flipper looked strange. The turtle had never seen anything quite like it, but he couldn't get close enough to really look it over.

"It's okay, take a rest and let the healing begin," the manatee continued. "This is where the man-tide rights its wrongs. This is where they mend their ways. I'm Naillij."

"Nice to meet you," the turtle mumbled, not convinced all this was actually happening. The place where the man-tide rights its wrongs seemed a little hard for the endangered turtle to swallow. Still, he indulged Naillij, "Name's Gilgongo."

"It's a genuine pleasure," the manatee cooed.

Dark, quiet, uncertain. It was a week both Norton and Cariam wanted to forget, but probably never would. At first, they expected to be killed. When that didn't happen they thought they'd be left to die, but that didn't happen either. Ultimately, they found themselves swimming in small separate containers, which somehow had wound up together on the other side of the planet. One glance into the night sky and Norton knew where they were located relative to Makoona, but that was all he knew about their mysterious location.

The lid popped partially off. Clouds appeared in the crack. Putting his suction power to good use, Cariam climbed up the side of the container. He turned white, shoved one of his eyes into the opening and saw a strange new world. A land world and a sea world both seemed to meet on this spot. There was the ocean, and there was the land. There was sea life, and there was man-tide. The two seemed to share the space, but it was obvious who was in charge. Cariam took mental notes of everything he saw.

The octopus slipped from the rim when one of the man-tide reached down and gently pushed him back into the water. As soon as the temperature in the container matched the temperature in the massive tank, the two refugees from Makoona were dropped into their new home. Cariam squeezed his siphon, shooting himself deep into the unfamiliar coral and hunkered down. A few fins in front of him Norton buried himself in the sand. They sat in silence, seeing the same things, thinking the same thoughts and trying to understand what was happening to them. There were fish everywhere, but it wasn't like the reef. What was the connection between these fish and the man-tide? They concluded that the fish were of the sea, but many were not of Makoona or even the Ocean of Peace. Certainly, the gazer and the octopus had heard of other reefs, other oceans. Fish who migrated or journeyed often returned to the reef with incredible stories of other creatures and exotic places. But no one had ever described anything like this. Could this be a place from which no fish returned? They were in a real pickerel. Norton and Cariam waited and watched — a tried and true practice of fish the world over. For the first time, they were in a totally foreign environment. Where was the shelter? Where was the prey? And more importantly, where were the predators?

The coral was plentiful, but as Cariam slid under what appeared to be a rocky outcrop, encrusted with sponge and coral, he could see the branches were dead. The polyps had no life. This dead coral could provide cover, but that was all. Sharks circled the surface. A pair of barracuda, jacks, tuna, several species unknown to him, a flounder, trigger fish and others shared the tank.

Cariam smelled them first, Norton a moment later. There were eels, morays, sharing the coral. The octopus climbed deeper into the imitation coral. Any one of the predators in the tank could have snapped him up in an instant. As the sharks and 'cudas swam within fins of Norton and Cariam, none of them seemed interested. There was a sleepy disinterest in their eyes. The octopus wondered whether it was some type of charade, an attempt to lure him into a sense of false security. Were these predators imposters, like the counterfeit coral?

On the real reef, there were so many colors and shapes, alive and growing. Coral and fish combined to create a tableau that was absolutely divine, not only in its appearance, but in its balance and harmony as well. It was the spirit. On the real reef, creatures lived inside the spirit, and were part of it. This tank of the man-tide was an insult, a demented diorama that disgusted the gazer and the octopus.

"Are you okay?" Norton asked.

"I'm from the reef, I have no problem with crowds. It's the walls I'm having trouble with. We've entered a very strange world," Cariam whispered. And just when the octopus was about to venture beyond the confines of his cover, a scalloped hammerhead dropped down in front of him. It was agitated, swimming in short bursts, twisting its head from side to side. Cariam knew all too well that between the eyes, across the front of its head, the shark had nerves that could sense and locate the electrical pulse of life found in all of Seaqoyit's creations. No matter how still one remained, whether covered by sand, rocks or weed, if a hammerhead really tried, it could find anything. This one was on the prowl. In this tank the two friends might be able to swim, but they could not hide.

A majestic eagle-ray cast a wide shadow as it rose from the sand and searched the surface. It, too, looked ready to hunt. Cariam climbed out of the coral branches, turned a dull tan and perched himself to get a better view. He wrapped three arms around the make-shift coral and spread three more mimicking the shape and the texture of the branches that surrounded him. A grouper galloped around the lifeless stand, also agitated. A snook snapped at a small snapper. A moray emerged from a hole and brandished its menacing mouth. Neither of the former Makoonan residents had ever seen so many predators in such a small space so interested in eating. It was a multi-species feeding frenzy. To add to the confusion, there was no shortage of small docile candidates and smaller predators swimming around that could have easily been gobbled up, yet they weren't. The only logical conclusion that Norton and Cariam could come up with was that a massive massacre was about to take place.

"Don't get too worked up. You're still thinking ocean. This happens in here all the time. It's a tank thing." A fish was speaking to them softly. "I'm down here, at the base."

Cariam slowly looked down. Norton gently tilted his head. Neither wanted to give away their position. They scoured the sediment until they spotted him. A flounder, unlike any they had seen before, was partially buried in the sand, not far from Norton. It matched the sand perfectly and had subtle blue rings marking its entire body.

"Just stay where you are and you guys will do fine. Get in the way of those lunatics and you'll end up as an appetizer."

"What's going on?" Norton asked.

"Where are we?" Cariam added.

"First things first. Let's survive this moment... see if we can catch a bite or two... then I'll answer all your questions. For now, do what I do."

"But you're not doing anything," the octopus protested.

"Precisely," the sole countered.

Then the feeding began. The food fell from above. A primordial display, a dangerous dance had somehow replaced the actual hunt. It was a mass mutilation unlike anything on Makoona. Yet there was no hunt, no chase, no kill. The food was already dead and quite cold. None of the fish in the tank were harmed. While the larger, more aggressive fish tore at the food that fell into the water, pieces sank below the predatorial feeding line. They were then snapped up by silver slashing jacks and blues, and others who were less lethal, but equally interested. As the remnants descended further, a third wave of feeders crept out of the coral and scavenged to their hearts' content. Then, as suddenly as it began, the feeding was over. The ravenous ray, the gluttonous grouper, the hungry hammerhead, the tense tuna all settled back into their mindless swim. Back and forth across the sand, over the coral.

Cariam began to understand. They were in a sea with walls, although when Cariam considered the dimensions of the ocean, this was little more than a glorified tidal pool. There had been walls on Makoona, great balustrades of rock and coral, but always there was a way around, a way over, a way under. Neither Norton nor Cariam could spy any cracks in these walls.

The flounder who emerged to feed strayed from their shelter with surprising bravado. It seemed as if once feeding was over, these predators who lived in such close proximity would not hurt them, were not interested in them. They were given food, plenty of it, and in return had no need to eat each other.

What the octopus and the gazer saw before them was the distorted vision of a reef, but it was not a reef. The balance, the behavior, the coral… it wasn't real. This was the man-tide's reef, not Seaqoyit's. Feeding, for instance, had become an empty ritual. It had lost its edge, its life. It had become a performance. But, Norton and Cariam wondered, a performance for whom?

There was, however, one element that was remarkably real: The water. The water within the tank was every bit as real as the water beyond the walls. No creature was more sensitive to this than the octopus. Based solely on minute chemical traces that touched his skin, he could tell exactly what creatures shared this reef. His epidermis functioned like a giant tongue. Cariam could literally taste the water over his entire body. And this water tasted pretty true, pretty blue.

In fact, the water in all the tanks in SeaTopia was pumped in directly from the ocean no more than two hundred yards away. While this water had a different aftertaste than Cariam's own Ocean of Peace, it was, no doubt, the real thing. The water was fresh, alive. It somehow took the edge off everything else that was not.

Cariam allowed the wake of the passing fish to wash over him. It was the octopus's way of taking a *sense-us*. And whatever Cariam didn't taste, Norton usually saw. In a short time they had a very good idea of just who was in this community.

A large bull shark passed overhead, its small eyes locked trancelike on the tailfin of the hammerhead just ahead of it. The bull continued on its way, but an emissary dropped out from behind its gills. A remora, a whitefin sharksucker, settled in the sand next to Norton. The peacock flounder quietly slipped away.

"Welcome to Quala. We've never had a gazer before. That is what you are, right?"

Norton smiled at the remora who scanned the coral.

"Never had an octopus, wherever he is, living among us

either. My name's Seacuesea. On behalf of the large predators, I'm here to welcome you to Quala. I'll try to answer your questions. I'm sure you have plenty. And, I can also fill you in on some of the ways we do things around here."

"You mean the rules?" Norton surmised.

"Well, you could call them that, but we prefer to refer to them as 'mutually benefishial practices for creatures sharing shallow water,'" the remora spawned a warm trusting grin. "And there is an octopus somewhere around here, isn't there?"

Norton shrugged his large pectoral fins.

"I'm just trying to avoid doing this a second time."

"Before you give me the rules — " Norton interrupted.

Seacuesea tilted his head and widened his eyes as if there was something wrong with the statement.

" — I mean 'mutually benefishal shallow stuff…'"

"Close enough," the remora nodded.

"Could you tell me where I am?"

"Your name?"

"I'm Norton. And, yes, I'm a gazer."

"I'll bet you're also from the Ocean of Peace?"

Norton nodded.

"They don't usually mix us… different salinity and that sort of thing…but sometimes it does happen. Anywave, now you are in Quala. The man-tide keep us here. They give us everything. We are contained, but there are benefits, as you will learn. Some have been here forever, some have not… like you and your friend… Could you get him to come over here?"

"He's kinda tough to locate sometimes," Norton said, knowing when to clam up.

"I see. You will not leave here, so you'd be best served to think of Quala as home. The sooner you do that, the more enjoyable your days will become."

"You mentioned that 'mutually benefishial' thing?"

"Yes, yes. There are only three practices we must all adhere to. First, accept the situation. Go with the flow. It will go better for you and those around you if you do. Second, know your place. That means you feed after the larger predators. There is plenty for everyone if you wait your turn. And, we like to keep the predators calm. Keep a respectable distance at all times."

"Interesting rule, coming from a remora," Norton pointed out.

"I'm still allowed to be a remora, so my respectable distance is 'attached.' Also, in matters of debate, the predators will decide." Seacuesea waited for the gazer's acknowledgement.

"Okay…"

"The last practice is the most important." The remora looked directly into Norton's eyes, emphasizing the point. "Obey the first two practices. As long as you do, no predator will harm you. They are, after all, very well fed."

"It depends how you define 'well fed'," Norton quipped, taking a jab at the man-tide's version of feeding.

"That's precisely what I'm talking about. Not a very healthy attitude. They're fed well enough that the predators have no interest in, or need for, your scales. Wouldn't you rather be their chum than chum?"

Once again, Norton nodded.

"We live by the guidelines that have served us well."

A shadow passed overhead. Seacuesea looked up, smiled and said, "There's my ride." He swam up and attached himself to the lumbering bull shark. "I'm glad we had this little chat. Nice to meet you. Say hello to your friend for me."

Norton had no need to deliver the welcome to Cariam. The octopus had heard every word. He was the orange sponge sitting behind the remora. Both Norton and Cariam were surprised that the fish could not locate the octopus. Perhaps those who lived in the tanks for long periods lost some of the abilities the spirit had bestowed upon them.

Samantha had finished both her dinner and her homework. The rest of the evening was hers. And just as her daily obligations had ended, so had the dolphins'. Their last show was over at 4:40 p.m. Then they ate. Samantha usually arrived around 5 p.m. By then all the visitors and handlers were gone. She loved sitting alone in SeaTopia's amphitheater. But Samantha wasn't really alone. After all, there were three dolphins. The solitary visitor understood that the *real* show was the one the dolphins put on after everyone else had wandered away. She sat in the front row, as if it was the first pew in a chapel, sketching and scribbling into a tattered notebook that, like the backpack, had a cover commemorating the television show, *Flipper*. The notebook and its contents were private, a dream that belonged to Samantha.

Lately, Samantha had begun to reach into the tank. She could mimic some of the signals of the handlers and then reward the dolphins with enthusiastic praise in the form of scratches, strokes and the occasional hug. It wasn't as filling as a mullet, but the dolphins seemed to get nourishment just the same. They understood that was all Samantha had to give, which was fine, because enthusiastic clicks, squeaks, whistles and head shaking smiles were all they had to give Samantha — a fair trade between mutual admirers.

Occasionally she found a stray basketball beneath the blue benches that circled the tank. Samantha would throw the ball to her three friends, who would catch the ball in their mouths and, laughing, toss it back to her. The three dolphins were the best baby-sitters Samantha could imagine. When she embraced them she felt a warmth, a genuine affection that she had never received from another human.

Samantha drifted off into scenes from her favorite movie, a film she guessed that no one on the planet, other than she, would claim as their favorite flick, *The Incredible Mr. Limpet*, starring Don Knotts. She often felt just like Henry Limpet, who wondered if he might be happier if he could live as a fish. When the movie played in a small revival cinema a few towns over, Samantha had taken the bus there every night for two weeks to see back to back showings. She'd even catch it now and then on television. Even on the small screen, in fuzzy black and white, *Limpet* worked its magic. For some reason, the film spoke to her. Part of her wished she could turn into a dolphin and join her friends in the water, where she romanticized life was simple, real and pure.

Just as the girl marveled at the dolphins, they felt connected to her. She was not like the mass of man-tide who arrived and disappeared like the surf. She was not like the trainers who had expectations and rules. Samantha was a friend. Janee, the mother, shared the water with Niv and Nhoj, her two sons. Although only Nhoj was born out of the tank, both brothers had been fathered by Onaro, Janee's mate in the sea.

By man-tide standards, the three dolphins lived a very comfortable life. They were well-cared for and active, putting on athletic and intellectual displays everyday. Their health was monitored. They had each other for company. The dolphins seemed very well situated.

But like the other creatures housed in SeaTopia, the dolphins missed the wild. The incredible array of survival skills that the spirit-fish had given them withered in the water of the tank. The hunt, the chase, the conquest, the games and the journeys were no longer needed, and had been replaced by scheduled fun and games with the man-tide. While there were absolute moments of fun, there was no danger or socialization and little discovery, especially once one mastered the simple tricks and signals that seemed to please their keepers, with no currents, tides, new grounds or travel, this was not a life any self-respecting dolphin would choose. Janee's dorsal fin, which once rose prominently, regally, now sagged and drooped, no longer tested against the strong currents of the open ocean.

To make matters worse from the dolphins' perspective, the

tanks at SeaTopia were situated right on the beach. Janee, whose name meant "gift of the sea," and her two sons could hear the surf rise and fall, the cackles and squeals of birds plundering bait-fish just off shore. They could smell salt in the wet air. The water pumped into their tanks from the sea, caressed their tongues and teased them with tastes of home. And when they leapt into the air, above the walls of the tank, performing some trick, they could see the ocean — their ocean — without any hope of ever returning.

Janee never told Niv or Nhoj, but there were times when she threw herself into the air looking out beyond the bleachers and thought she saw, out there somewhere, her pod. She called to them every time she breached the surface and flew above the bar or through the hoop that hung across the tank. She had crazy thoughts that she could see Onaro, her mate. But she knew he was gone. They would never see the sea, never be a family, again.

Whatever she felt, Janee knew it was worse for her two sons. At least she had memories. During quiet moments she would let her mind drift back across the sand into the ocean of her birth. She was carried away by the mental images of places she had seen, others she had known. Her favorite thoughts, the ones she called on most often, were the memories of being young with Onaro. Together, it seemed, the water had been wetter, the clouds softer, and there was so much more life in being alive. With their sons swimming beside them, the feelings she and Onaro shared would have become even more profound. Sadly, they had never swum as a family and almost certainly never would.

It tore at Janee that her sons were denied experiences all living creatures were entitled to, that they had never known life outside the tanks. Their genetic design, unsurpassed in the sea, unlike any other mammal, would not be part of the balance. Her children would not live the lives of dolphins. She wasn't sure whether to tell her sons stories of the sea, or withhold them. Janee tried to ease her worries by telling herself that they wouldn't miss what they'd never had. In their situation, not knowing the sea might actually be a blessing.

The man-tide wouldn't let them go hungry or get sick. They tended to all their ailments and provided for many needs. On one fin, they were safe where they were, but on the other fin, that was part of the problem. They were, perhaps, too safe.

Niv, the younger of her sons, had been born in the tanks shortly after Janee arrived. He was, at times, quiet and contemplative. He liked moments alone. He was focused and occasionally more serious than a young dolphin needed to be. He had never met his father, never rubbed against a reef, or chased mullet with other youngsters. Yet he did have a glow, a freedom of spirit that not even captivity could extinguish. There was a joker, a prankster, a performer inside the young dolphin.

Nhoj was the elder of the two. He had a wild streak in him that came from the wild, although he only lived in the sea for a short time. Nhoj liked to pretend that he was far more experienced in the ways of the water than he actually was, constantly telling both his mother and his brother how things really were "out there." He told tales of heroism and adventure that had only happened in his mind. Nevertheless, his mother and Niv enjoyed the fintastic tales.

Whatever the situation might have been, Janee had her sons. It was enough. It would have to be.

The Comoros fishermen laid their collection of business cards on a wobbly table in the local hotel. They flipped through the small rectangles until they came across the name Dave Lackland, Senior Aquarist, SeaTopia. Several fishermen nodded. They remembered Dave. His pockets were not the deepest, but of all the outsiders they encountered, he was the most understanding, the least offensive. He was not *mzungus*. He did not encourage locals to hook canths, but whenever a canth did appear, Dave was sure to be fascinated. The cadaver of the coelacanth would be offered to him first. If Dave wasn't interested, then the rest of the scientists could bid for the lifeless specimen.

After the phone call, the fishermen returned to the holding tank, pleased Dave remembered them, and thrilled he would purchase the fish for a good price. Although the money had not even left SeaTopia, the fishermen were already planning how to spend their newly found riches. They did have one task left to perform. Lackland demanded that they make room in a freezer somewhere for the coelacanth. He made it clear that SeaTopia would not write a check for a rotten, decomposing carcass. He wanted a pristinely preserved coelacanth. Dave had no idea just how well preserved the specimen would be.

When the fishermen arrived at the tank, the coelacanth was gone. The other two carcasses that were dumped in the tank to cool were still there, but the coelacanth had somehow disappeared. As they searched the grounds looking for clues to solve the apparent theft, one of the men laughed and yelled, "Look! Look at this!"

Hunkered down in the grotto, in the darkest quietest corner of the tank, Maputa watched them. She was alive. Although she had entered the mouth of death's cave, several hours in the tank had revived her. The fishermen no longer had a lifeless specimen. They now had the only living coelacanth ever in captivity in the world. It was a priceless jewel of the sea, quite a coup for the relatively unknown aquarium.

Ahamadi Abdallah, the man who had caught the fish and made the deal with SeaTopia, turned to his assistant, Souha, and said, "Looks like Dave bought a very fresh fish. Do you think he still wants us to freeze it?"

One man didn't laugh. "A dead coelacanth was sold," he said. "This one is alive."

The leader stroked his thick beard and shook his head. "This is Dave's fish. If he bought a live fish and it died, we wouldn't return his money. So, if he buys a dead fish and it rises, it is his gain. If SeaTopia would like to pay us something extra for bringing it back to life, I would be happy to accept the tribute."

"We are not permitted to catch live coelacanths," another fisherman whispered.

"What has happened is a miracle. It was not alive when we caught it. You are all witnesses. And it was not alive when we sold it. I would like my money, so I believe this fish, for better or worse, is now SeaTopia's problem."

Maputa had no idea what was happening to her. Again she was being handled and removed. Without her family, without her sea, she was confused and depressed, so she allowed the tide of destiny to carry her wherever she was meant to go.

Eventually, though she didn't fully understand it, she wound up in a custom-made tank at SeaTopia. When Dave realized the coelacanth was alive, he arranged for one of America's few coelacanth experts, Dr. Don Dorfman from Monmouth University, to create and construct a habitat that would make Maputa comfortable in her new surroundings. For Dorfman it was the chance of a lifetime, a test to see if he really understood the creature he had studied for his entire professional life. His goal, his mandate, was to recreate the Comoros, so she could return home without ever leaving SeaTopia.

When she finally arrived at the aquarium and Dorfman saw her in the bright sterile holding tank, the professor almost cried. He reached into the water, ignoring the teeth set in the monstrous jaw, and stroked the coelacanth. The large armor-like scales, which others would point to and grimace, felt like a favored pet's shiny coat under the biologist's fingers. He stroked the fish and whispered, "Welcome to the twentieth century."

Maputa did not move. The hand did not repulse her. This hand, she felt, was not going to hurt her. This hand was not like the other hands. Dorfman reassured the fish, "The first thing we're going to do is get you out of this temporary tank and put you in something a little more fitting for a fish of your pedigree." The professor reached his other hand to the dimmer switch and brought the lights down to a level that would be more in keeping with the deep water Maputa was used to.

Before the coelacanth had arrived, the director and the scientist appropriated a tank that had two levels to which they added a third level on top. The tank was lined with a two-way mirror so patrons could see in but the canth could not see out. Two caves were built: One on level one, the other on level two. Both had windows in the rear. The inside of the tank was dimly lit with red light, although there were moments when daylight would pass over the surface. The water pressure was increased, the temperature decreased and the salinity controlled to mimic the water of the Comoros.

SeaTopia was preparing for a very special guest. Maputa was a foreign dignitary more rare in captivity that the Great Panda or Mountain Gorilla. And when they were finally prepared to open the exhibit, the coelacanth would make headlines. Not to mention millions.

As soon as the remora was out of sight, the flounder emerged from the sand. "So you've been visited by Seacusea. The messenger has arrived."

Cariam slid down a coral branch, buried himself at the base of the stalk and morphed into a sandy tan, flecked with brown streaks. "Didn't leave much of a message. Hello, here are the rules."

The flounder looked anxious. "Keep two things in mind, my friends. First, when the remora speaks, always remember who he is speaking for. Also," the sole wriggled his way a little deeper into the sand and colored himself a shade darker, "the coral has ears. Think carefully about what you say out loud in here."

The gazer and the octopus glanced at each other. "So, really," Cariam began, "what that remora said was true? If we stay quiet and out of the way, we'll get our food — "

" — And won't become theirs?" Norton added.

"Yes," the sole sneered, "that's what I'm talking about." And then, as if he had become a different fish, continued, "You'll get used to it. It's really not too bad." The fish seemed to be hurrying away.

Norton noticed the dim shadow of a barracuda hanging motionless on the surface above the coral. He followed the sole's lead and replied merrily, "Yeah, life here sounds pretty sweet. Thanks for the welcome, buddy. Hey, what's your name?"

"Everyone calls me Finbar."

"See ya around," Cariam called.

As he disappeared behind a cement rendition of an orange sponge, the flounder said, "In a place like this, you can count on it."

Norton and Cariam drifted to the most remote spot they could find, a private corner far from the central stand of coral. They came to a wall that ran the entire perimeter of the tank. Together, they followed the balustrade's contours until they realized that finding an isolated spot might be difficult. Continuing on their quest, they smiled and waved at passing fish along the way. A spotted eagle ray glided in for a friendly look, nodded and went on its way. A trio of curious croakers also swam by for a peek at the new arrivals.

Norton turned to speak to Cariam. The octopus was gone. The gazer stuffed himself into the sand and scanned the water. He whispered, "Cariam... Cariam... where are you?"

Above the sand, a few fins up the man-tide's wall, a long sucker-covered arm, tinted sky blue, emerged. It came out of no where. There was only an arm. The gazer wondered if something had torn the appendage from Cariam. It protruded from the flat smooth wall, all by itself, waving with the undulating water. Norton tried to locate the rest of his friend. Would it be too late to help? Whose belly was he in? Would he be next? The gazer muttered to himself, "Yeah, predators don't prey in here. Tell that to Cariam." Norton's friend was gone.

Then something strange happened. The arm started to move independently of the water's flow. It curled slowly upward and inward, upward and inward, as if beckoning to Norton. The fish was both mesmerized and repulsed by the sight. Cariam was gone, and yet, his dismembered arm clung to life. Norton waited for one of the passing fish to notice it and snap it up as a quick treat. The blue arm curled again, and again. Then an octopus emerged from the flat wall and hissed, "Norton, get up here!"

It was Cariam! Norton burst from the sand. He nuzzled the arm and finbraced his friend. "Spirit be praised! You're alive! You haven't been eaten!"

Cariam slapped a sucker onto the fish's flank, pulling him into a hole in the wall. "If you don't clam down, we might just get eaten."

"But I thought you were gone."

"I found this." Three blue arms pointed to a tight little tunnel. Norton and Cariam sat inside the entrance. Since he had no bones, the octopus could move through the tunnel quite easily. It was a little harder for Norton, but the stout fish managed to squeeze his way along. Eventually, the tunnel opened into another tank, somewhat smaller than the one they had left. This one also had coral, but it was the real thing. It was alive. Cariam stroked the ridges of a healthy porous coral cup. It was electric red. After a second or two he became the same electric red, folded his arms over his head and contracted his skin to mimic the texture of the single coral cup. And then there were two.

Norton knew just what this meant. He dug his body into the sand. This was where the two would speak openly to each other. "What do you think this is?" Norton began.

"I don't know."

Fish swam throughout the tank. There was a shortnose batfish, a toadfish, a striated frogfish, several oysters, a pair of seahorses, an angelfish, a few small triggers, a cave bass, a pygmy filefish, and a spotted drum. Some goby cleaners had set up shop over a large flat rock. There were anemones, complete with clownfish, sponges, algae and a spattering of marine plants also in the tank. The water was filled with small reef fish. Apparently, the tunnel connected the two communities, allowing the smaller residents to pass from one tank into the other.

The striated frogfish ambled over toward the coral cups. It pecked and snapped at particles caught in the ridges of the genuine specimen. It enjoyed a quiet little snack until it pecked at the imposter coral. The octopus turned white and uncoiled. Instantly, he liked the frogfish, who was already busy apologizing.

"I'm so sorry. I didn't know the man-tide had placed an octopus among us. You fooled me so completely. I never suspected that the coral was actually an octopus. My, you're talented."

And that was why Cariam liked the frogfish instantly. There is no higher compliment one can give an octopus than mistaking it for the thing it is mimicking. And there's no better way to deliver the compliment than to actually bite the octopus because you're so fully fooled.

Norton also liked the frogfish, but for a different reason. Norton found her to be quite attractive. They both shared the highly placed, wide, down-turned mouth. Surely, a sign of intelligence. Their bodies had a similar funnel-like shape. But the striated frogfish was much more decorative. It was frilly, elaborate. This particular one was so up front and in your scales. And while almost all of the fish Cariam and Norton had seen were not of their ocean, they had known frogfish on Makoona.

"It's been ages since I've seen an octopus. I've forgotten how incredible your kind is. I'm almost happy to see you. But, of course, that would be shellfish of me."

"That's okay. Although the man-tide did bring us here, we

arrived in this particular tank by our own doing."

"Ah, the tunnel."

Cariam nodded.

"I generally stay here, but some fish commute from one tank to the other. Excuse me, did you say 'we?' Is there another octopus?"

"Well..."

"Oh, don't tell me. I can find it."

"Actually..."

"No, no, no. I can do this! Okay, hot or cold?"

"What?"

"Am I hot or cold?"

"Uhhh. Red hot."

"I knew it! Let's see. The octopus is right... there!" The frogfish threw herself at a yellow sponge. It bent over and popped back up. "Right. That's been there for three years. Okay, hot or cold?"

"Look, you're not gonna find another oct — "

"I found you, didn't I?"

"Not really. You thought you found a coral cup."

"Merely a tentacality. Stop splitting scales. I found you and I'll find the other octopus too."

"It's a gazer."

"The octopus has disguised himself as a gazer? The only octopus that I've seen disguise itself as a gazer is a Wonderpus. You brought a Wonderpus with you disguised as a gazer?"

"No, I brought a gazer with me disguised as — "

"A Wonderpus? I didn't know gazers could do that."

"No! *It's a gazer.* A *gazer.* Not disguised as anything. Just a GAZER!"

Then both the frogfish and Cariam heard a muffled mumble. A ripple and some small bubbles rose from beneath the frogfish. "Oh, excuse me," she said reflexively. The octopus gently moved her to the side and Norton emerged from the sand. The frogfish looked at Norton, turned to Cariam and said, "Red hot?"

The octopus grinned, "You were on top of him."

"Sorry," the fish apologized. It wasn't necessary. In Norton's eyes, she could do no wrong. There were creases in the scales and skin that surrounded her eyes, evidence that she smiled a lot. Norton appreciated that quality. And so, when he saw her face, it made him smile too. "Hi, I'm Norton."

"I'm Flow."

The moment was interrupted when Cariam asked, "So, who rules *this* water?"

"Who rules?"

"Well, the predators seem to be in charge of the place we just left. What goes on here? You have some scorpion fish who's in charge?"

Flow straightened up. "Well, there is a scorpion fish, but she doesn't rule. And there are certainly some fishlosophies that most of us share, but I can assure you that no one fish, or group of fish for that matter, makes the rules here. The only rules we try to follow are those of the spirit, and there's even some disagreement there."

"Do you like it here?" Norton asked.

"Like it? Well, I like this place better than the one you just came from, but no, I don't like it here. I'd rather be out there."

"Who wouldn't?" the octopus asked rhetorically.

The frogfish tilted her head, raised a fin and grinned. "I never really considered it before, but now that you mention it, there is one."

"One who wouldn't like it better out there?" Cariam quizzed.

"I mean one who likes it in here. Pagre, the angelfish."

"Is he a true angelfish?" Norton asked. Like all fishtians, the gazer had heard of angelfish sent by the spirit. They were often connected. Some had missions; some had insight; some had visions; some even spoke directly with Seaqoyit. And some had all of these blessings. Neither Norton nor his friend had ever actually met a true angelfish. This was the last place they expected to see one.

"You tell me if he's a true angelfish. He's right over there. Come on, I'll introduce you."

When Flow suggested that Cariam and Norton introduce themselves to Pagre the angelfish, the two had assumed it would entail a bit of a journey, forgetting that in the tanks nothing, save freedom, was ever very far away. So they were somewhat surprised when the frogfish led them past a golden zoanthid growing out of a red boring sponge and there, only a few fins from where they had been talking, a solitary angelfish was pecking through some stones and coral that lined the base of the reef. Sun beams twisted and danced across the fish's scales as he stirred the water. The sediment sparkled, rising and falling in the controlled turbulence.

The angel was a hybrid, the result of a Queen Angel's union with a Blue Angel. Their offspring, Pagre, was one of a kind. He had his mother's bright yellow tailfin, his father's pale blue eyes and lips, and a unique blue-green mottled body that was all his own. The fish's vibrant scales were every bit as striking as the coral that framed him. And for a moment, watching him occupied in his chores, it was easy to forget that they were all sea-questered by the wall beyond the coral.

Flow nodded to Pagre and swam closer. The two visitors followed, realizing that the angelfish was quite large, among the biggest either had ever seen. Captivity seemed to agree with him. In spite of his size, the creature's aura was so gentle, so calm that its bulk almost passed unnoticed.

Pagre knew he was being watched. After years of living in a tank, he had gotten comfortable with the reefality that, short of stuffing himself into some constricting coral crack, he would always be on display to those who lived around him. However, this did not concern Pagre. He was one of those very special angelfish who had found the spirit. He was living with something much larger than anything that shared his tank. While others swam circles in the sterile salt water, he swam in the spirit. And yet, he did not perform miracles, nor did he know all the answers.

Pagre raised his head, slowed his chewing and greeted the frogfish. Touching fins, he said, "What it is."

"What it was," his friend countered solemnly.

"What it shall be." Pagre smiled knowingly. Then he looked past Flow and said, "Look what the catfish dragged in. The octopus and the gazer. I've heard. Word travels fast in a tank."

The newcomers nodded.

Norton began. "Since you're an angelfish, could you answer a question I've always had?"

"I'll try."

"What do fishtians mean by the 'holy' spirit?"

"Norton!" Flow exclaimed.

"I'm just asking."

Pagre smiled. "If you prayed to the 'holy' spirit when the man-tide picked you up in a net or put you in a tank, then you wouldn't be here right now."

"Is he serious?" the gazer said to Flow. "What I mean — " Norton stopped in mid-sentence, thought for a moment, then smiled. "Wait. I get it. If I believed in the *holey* spirit, there'd be holes in the nets and holes in the walls so I could leave, right?"

"You got it," Pagre replied.

"Was that a stupid question?" the gazer guessed.

"No more stupid than my answer."

The foursome lounged around the coral comfortably. After a little while, Norton asked, "Flow says you're happy to be here. How can that be? Wouldn't you rather be in the sea?"

"Well, yes, I would rather be in the sea, if it were my choice. But I take refuge under Seaqoyit's fins. And behold," Pagre gestured to include all of SeaTopia, "everything becomes new."

Cariam turned a confused purple. "You lost me."

"No, I think I'm finding you. Let me explain. By giving it all up to the spirit, this captivity and everything beyond my control, without ever leaving, I am freed."

Norton nodded. "I'm not usually one to cut to the chase. As a gazer, I don't like chases. I'd rather remain unnoticed. But this one time, let me cut to the chase and ask you, do you really speak to Seaqoyit?"

"Well," the angel answered, "in the spirit of cutting to the chase, the short answer is, yes. But really, anyone can talk to Seaqoyit. You don't need to be an angel."

"But does the spirit talk to you?" Norton pressed.

Cariam was looking around, getting bored, but the gazer was fascinated.

Pagre continued, "Again, the short answer is, yes. But again, anyone can do it."

When the sun dipped below the rim of the wall, Cariam said, "We'll see you later. Gonna mingle a bit more before the day's over."

"Yeah," Norton added, "it's fin and grin time for the new fish on the reef."

Flow giggled, "I think your octopus friend might have a little trouble with the fin part."

"Not me," Cariam countered, waving his eight appendages proudly, "I am armed to charm." He reached out and shook Flow, Pagre and Norton's fins simultaneously.

"Charming," Norton noted.

After the two pairs parted waves, Pagre turned to Flow and spoke quietly. "The spirit hath said, 'I will never leave thee, nor forsake thee. So that we may boldly say, "The spirit is my helper, and will not fear what man shall do unto me."

"A-fish," Flow whispered, "A-fish."

Gilgongo was recovering nicely. He swam in circles around the small sparse tank reflecting on how the man-tide had caused his injuries and yet the man-tide treated his wounds. The turtle recalled a funny little bird, a petrel who had arrived on a patch of seaweed Gilgongo shared with his mother, brothers and sisters when he was a youngster. After a brutal storm, the strange bird, unlike any he had ever seen before, landed on the turtles' green patch. The injured bird, Lupé, stayed with them while Gilgongo's mother helped him regain his health. At the moment, Gilgongo felt like Lupé when he was injured on the seaweed: In good company, but still trapped and vulnerable. The turtle wondered, if he was finally healed, would he be able to continue his migration, just as Lupé had done. Gilgongo stretched his head out of the water, looked over the grounds of SeaTopia and doubted that his journey would continue.

The turtle had made a friend. The manatee in the next tank was also being helped by the man-tide. Her injuries were not unlike Gilgongo's. Both creatures now sported custom-made prosthetic latex flippers, which replaced the damaged flippers that had to be removed. Naillij's rear fluke had been amputated and replaced. Gilgongo's rear flipper, destroyed by fishing line that had cut and strangled the limb, had also been replaced.

The manatee and turtle spoke together as they swam lazy long circles. Neither could understand why the man-tide wouldn't be more careful initially, rather than be faced with all this bother later on.

Naillij said, "Reminds me of Retep, a manatee who shared a river with my family."

"What reminds you of Retep?" Gilgongo asked.

"The man-tide," she answered. "Retep was young, strong, smart, but very insecure. He ate all the eel grass in our range along the river. He ate the grass right down to its roots, until an entire feeding ground was bare. Everyone warned him not to do it, but to leave some so it would continue to grow and feed manatees forever.

"But Retep liked to do what he was told not to do. Then, when the grass was gone, he made an unnecessary, unbelievable effort to bring eel grass back to the area. In the end, he succeeded, but along the way he frustrated everyone around him, causing many to eat less and take risks to find other food. It was a bad thing. And it all could have been avoided if he had shown a little restraint early on."

"So why'd he do it? And how does that remind you of the man-tide?" the turtle asked.

"In my opinion, he did it to show everyone how important he was. He ate all the food and then brought it back. It was a show of power, a display of worth. And that, my green friend, is the man-tide."

"I still don't get you."

"Like Retep, the man-tide ignores the balance. In fact, they violate it. Then they come in and try to make it right. They show they are more powerful than the spirit by destroying the balance. And then they fool themselves into thinking that by bringing things back to where they should have been all along, they have restored the balance, righted the wrong, reaffirming their power. But the wrong has still happened. Maybe not to them, not to Retep, but to us."

"So," Gilgongo guessed, "in the end, the problem is that what Retep and the man-tide have done is only for themselves. But really, Naillij, they don't have to do anything. They could leave us with our problems."

"In most cases, they actually leave us with their problems. You're wrong, though, to think that they don't *have* to do anything. They have to solve a little piece of the problem. Then they convince themselves that they can do no wrong, because they can right any wrong they create. It's not really about compassion. It's about power."

"I hope you're wrong. I hope there is some compassion in the man-tide." Gilgongo laid his face against the net that separated him from the manatee. He whispered, "I looked into the eyes of the one who carried me here. I looked into the eyes of the one who joined him. Now, I'm no expert on the eyes of the man-tide, but I'd swear that I saw compassion."

"I know that look. And like you, I also hope it is compassion." Naillij lifted her prosthetic out of the water. "Not very attractive, is it?" the manatee lamented. "I mean, how many times have you seen a manatee with a rear flipper like this?"

Although he had seen several manatees along the intra-coastal, in canals and bays, Naillij was right. Gilgongo had never seen a manatee like her, or for that matter, a turtle like himself.

Ignoring the aesthetic of the prosthetic, the turtle answered, "I've never been one to worry about how others see me. I'll tell you what's finfinitely worse than the way these things look."

"What's that?"

"It's even less attractive to see a turtle swimming in a crazed circle, unable to eat because his hind flipper is infected and mutilated. Now that's unattractive."

"You have a point there."

"While I like the original a lot better," the turtle smiled, "at least I can swim pretty normally with this thing. It's not a bad fit at all."

"Is it *normal* for a turtle to be swimming in some little man-tide puddle, with some man-tide flipper attached to him? Is that normal?"

"Well," the slick green head rose above the surface, looked at the surroundings and dipped back below the water, "I'm thinking this puddle is only temporary. I'm going to be swimming on pretty soon. I got a plan."

While Gilgongo was correct that his current container was only a temporary reefality, he failed to realize that the man-tide also had plans for him. But perhaps there were other plans, bigger plans, that neither the turtle nor the man-tide had considered.

As Samantha watched Nohj and Niv playing spirited games in the water, she thought about how, to most people, dolphins were only interesting when they were doing tricks. When patrons did linger, Samantha often heard them say stupid things like, "I love dolphins. They're my favorite fish." She was amazed that people could *love* something, yet know so little about it and show so little interest in it. It was, she thought, just like the kind of love her mother gave to her.

Samantha knew what real love was. It was devotion. It was everyday. And it wasn't easy or convenient. She knew it, partly, because no one gave it to her. She also knew it because she loved Janee and her sons. The more she thought about these things, the harder she scribbled in her journal, writing furiously until she saw something she couldn't believe.

As the last group of patrons moved on to another tank of their 'favorite fish,' a boy about Samantha's age tossed a half-eaten hot dog, dripping with mustard and relish, into the tank. "Have a frank," was all he said. And then he walked away.

Samantha raced to the tank. The floating hot dog had already been noticed by Nohj, who was not one to pass up a meal of any type. He turned one-hundred-eighty degrees and moved in on the morsel. Had Nohj known that he faced competition for the snack, he would have snapped it up long before Samantha got to it. Samantha stretched over the rail. She clambered over the rail to the platform used by the staff during dolphin shows.

"Hey!" a male voice shouted from somewhere behind her. "That's off limits!"

Her feet hit the wet surface and she slid, lost her balance and fell into the tank, her arm reaching for the hot dog. Just before she sank below the water, her fingers closed around the floating frank.

She bobbed to the surface and began treading water. Nohj and Niv eagerly nosed her fist, hoping for the treat. Janee was also interested, but for a different reason. The humans who normally entered her water were known. This one was not. And like mothers everywhere, regardless of species, Janee approached with the intention of protecting her young, something she was very capable of doing.

"Hey, you!" A very angry staff member was on the platform now. He knelt down and grabbed the girl by the back of the shirt. She reached for the platform's edge and let him help her out of the water.

"What do you think you're doing?"

Samantha opened her hand. "I—"

Bert took one look at the piece of hot dog and said, "Just thought you'd save the dolphins? Are you crazy! You could'a been hurt—"

"What's going on here?"

Samantha looked up.

Another man, also wearing staff clothing and a name plate that said "Dave-phin" was at the rail of the tank. "Come on, you two, get out of there, you're upsetting the dolphins."

Samantha turned, horrified. Janee was between her children and the platform. Nhoj and Niv, still curious, were darting rapidly back and forth behind her clicking and whistling, clearly agitated.

Samantha stood silently as Bert told Dave what had happened. The fact that she was only trying to protect the dolphins was somehow lost on Bert.

"Are your parents here?"

Samantha shook her head. The cool evening air against her wet clothes and skin made her shiver. Dave thanked Bert and gave Samantha's shoulder a little squeeze. When she looked up at him, he winked and smiled. "Let's get you some dry clothes and then *you* can tell me why you wanted to swim with the dolphins."

In Dave's office, he rummaged through a locker until he came up with a clean shirt, a pair of socks and a pair of pants. He handed the clothes to Samantha. "Why don't you change. I'll be right back."

He waited outside for a few minutes, then knocked before opening the door again. The clothes were too big, but at least they were dry. Dave recognized the girl—he'd often seen her drifting through SeaTopia. She'd even been given a knickname by the staff. They called her 'Shortstripe', because like the shortstripe goby, she had a habit of cleaning things up, while most patrons tended to be slobs. The table Samantha ate her dinner at everyday was always spotless when she left.

"I'm sorry," Samantha offered.

"You know that was dangerous, right?"

She nodded. "I know. I saw the hot dog and I panicked." Samantha couldn't look at him. She was too embarrassed.

"Dolphins can be unpredictable with people they don't know. So, it would probably be a good idea if they got to know you before you went swimming with them again."

She snuck a look at Dave's face. Was he saying what she thought he was?

"I see you around here a lot. Your parents work?"

"My mom. She bought me a pass."

"I see." He paused, then let out a sigh. "Let's dry those clothes. There's a dryer in the trainer's locker room."

"Are you going to call my mother?"

"Nope. But I am going to make you do something."

"What?"

"How'd you like a job?"

"You mean as a trainer?"

"Well, not exactly…"

Chapter Three
T'anks for the Memories...

Dave did not make the trip to the Comoros personally. He had too much to do to prepare SeaTopia for Maputa's arrival. The director called a friend of his, Dr. Don Dorfman, an ichthyologist at Monmouth University in New Jersey. The professor had devoted his career, as well as much of his personal life, to studying pre-historic type fish, and the traits that had survived. His specialty was the coelacanth. The old professor knew the creature and the Comoros, having accompanied Dave's team there a few years earlier. The former student was confident that his mentor could get Maputa safely to SeaTopia.

Dr. Dorfman invited one of his colleagues to help with the job. Dr. Helen Campbell, of the University of Queensland, Australia, had been working with a population of coelacanths in Indonesia, a species separate from the Comoros canths. She knew both fish and had worked with the SeaTopia staff before. Unfortunately, Campbell was too involved with her own canths to aid the SeaTopia staff, so she sent one of her most capable assistants to help with Maputa.

Maputa arrived at SeaTopia healthy, but not so happy, although few people could actually gauge what her spirits were. Following a brief quarantine and some extensive examination, Maputa was introduced into her new home.

The cool dark water was certainly the most hospitable habitat she had encountered since she was removed from the sea. The caves were relaxing. The canth was relieved to finally stretch her fins. There was one other thing that made the ordeal a little more livable: Maputa had a friend with her, a stowaway who no one had detected. The little shrimp that joined her in the man-trap had slipped under a scale, crawled into a gill slit and managed to make the trip from the Comoros to SeaTopia. By now, Shareef and Maputa were as close as a blind shrimp and a goby. While one might think that a huge coelacanth and a minute shrimp had absolutely nothing in common, the two friends didn't see it that way. Both were incredibly old life forms with eons of history, instinct and experiences to share. They both also came from the same waters, so they knew many of the same fish and hangouts. Now they were both stuck in the same situation, so there was plenty to chat about, even though Shareef had not left a family and newly born pups behind. It was the first cold fact that separated the two. The other was that Shareef had chosen to take the plunge. Maputa had not.

Maputa tried to live her life as normally as possible. She spent her days in one of the two caves. In the evenings, she swam out and either circled the tank slowly, or floated in place, tilting her head toward the imagined depths, raising her unique caudal fin toward the surface, hovering, praying, thinking. She scanned the water and the sand for prey that wasn't there. The canth intentionally dulled her awareness. Softening the sharp edge needed for survival in the wild to enhance the illusion that she was not a prisoner. The less she expected, the less she would be disappointed.

When she prayed, the canth generally asked for three things. One was to understand why Seaqoyit had placed this burden on her. The second request she made was that her thoughts would somehow reach her family. Maputa prayed to the spirit that her children would grow to know that she loved them and that they would, in some small way, see the world around them through their mother's eyes; she prayed that Nilmah would remember her touch, her voice and what it was like to have their lives fused into one. Finally, her last request was that the spirit would protect the other canths, allowing them to continue undisturbed in the water that had been given to them during creation. All things considered, it was not a lot to ask.

Shareef developed a different daily routine. He spent his days on a quest for information. The shrimp had taken the ride and was going to learn as much as he could. He examined every nook and cranny of their tank. He made forays to the surface, slipped his eager eye-stalks above the water and watched the man-tide. Small enough to pass unnoticed, he was smart enough to piece together snippets of the situation he and Maputa were faced with. While the shrimp was certainly an adventurer, he still had every intention of surviving.

Shareef often ate when the coelacanth hovered in prayer. He would slip into her mouth and consume all the tasty bits that clung to her teeth and jaws. The shrimp would clean her gill rakers and slip through Maputa's gill covers, giving them the once over on his way out. The canth appreciated the cleaning and the shrimp never missed a meal. Even in the tank, the spirit's harmony could not be quelled.

Not long after they were introduced to their new home, Shareef noticed something about Maputa that caused him concern. His friend seemed depressed. She was disarmingly quiet, sullen, almost dormant.

"It's not healthy to be so unhappy, even if you do have good reason," the shrimp commented.

"Yes, I do have good reason," Maputa agreed to the latter contention.

"I'm speaking to you as a friend. This depression will only weaken you. And we need to be strong."

"Why must I be strong? To catch food? To protect my young from tiger sharks and giant squids? To protect *myself?* None of that matters in this dead water."

Desperate, Shareef grabbed for the one thing that might get to the canth. "If you are stronger, your prayers will be stronger."

Maputa opened her eyes and faced her friend. He had captured her attention.

Not a very religious creature, the shrimp improvised, "The spirit will see that you cannot be broken by what the man-tide has done. The spirit will know that your faith is strong. And the spirit will hear your prayers more clearly than if you had given up or doubted."

"If I doubted what?"

For an instant Shareef was taken aback by what he had said. It was not like him to be so spiritual. He wondered where the words came from. Then he responded to Maputa's question, saying, "If you doubted that the spirit-fish has a stronger will than the man-tide, that in the end the spirit will prevail."

"The spirit is stronger. I believe that," the canth said with conviction, a sign of strength that Shareef found encouraging. Maputa broke from her trance-like meditation. "I have not given up. I have merely slowed down."

"And why would you do that?"

"It makes this easier. The same water everyday. The same food. The same sand. The same rocks. The same, forgive me, faces. If I don't look at all this, if I transport myself home with prayers, if I concentrate on then rather than now... living in the past, it all becomes easier to endure."

"Just be careful, my friend," Shareef warned. "A time may come when you need to be alert, when you need to be ready. Especially if your spirit-fish is listening."

The coelacanth understood and nodded.

Like Shareef, Smitty had also noticed Maputa's melancholy. Putting decorative trim and other last minute improvements in place around the canth's tank, he took time to watch the ancient fish, marveling at its grace, size and beauty. One of the staff members, upon seeing Maputa for the fist time said, "Now that's one ugly fish!" Smitty couldn't disagree more. Even though he didn't have the science degree from a fancy university, no one had to teach him to appreciate what swam before him. The coelacanth was anything but ugly. It was unique, graceful. Smitty appreciated the ancient design that still held its own in the modern world. As hard as man tried to tame nature, to conquer it, this fish never gave it a thought. It did not run out of time, it ran with it—for three hundred sixty million years.

"And it is beautiful," Smitty thought. He designed wood cut-outs and other ornaments that accentuated the lines and the colors of the canth. He wanted the visitors to see what he saw. The oldest person in SeaTopia at the moment, Smitty had learned long ago that appearance was merely one small facet of beauty. Real beauty came from many other sources. No matter what anyone else said, Smitty saw the beauty of the canth. To him it was royalty, a pearl, a form of perfection. He liked this fish, but he liked them all.

Seeing Maputa emerge from her cave, he wondered what she had seen in her life, what she was thinking now. One of the main reasons Smitty enjoyed spending his golden years tinkering at SeaTopia was the opportunity to be surrounded by all the life. It was creation. It was God's work. And he was dedicating himself to all these creatures that had been touched by the hand of God. The canth that floated on the other side of the glass would have agreed with Smitty that all those in the tanks were touched by God, but she would have maintained that they were touched by a divine *fin* rather than a hand.

Neither the coelacanth's lineage, nor the turtle's evolution, challenged Smitty's conviction that God was the creator. It actually confirmed it. He put his tools down and looked at the tanks scattered across SeaTopia. He looked beyond them to the whispering surf and watched a Ghost Crab disappear under the boardwalk. He knew in his heart, without any doubt, this was the work of God. This diversity, this web of life, the incredible creatures, the harmony, evolution itself, was all the work of God. Scores of people came and went, he lamented, without ever taking it all in, without seeing how everything was connected to something larger—and to something smaller. That's what SeaTopia said to Smitty.

Bending down to pick up a level and a rubber mallet, he watched Maputa mouth her meal. It was nothing like the frenzy among the large fish in the big tank, or the smaller ones in the reef tank. Maputa swallowed the pieces that floated her way. There was no chase, no churning of water, no rustle of rubble. She ate her frozen fish with the enthusiasm of a child sitting at the dinner table, a plate of canned lima beans in front of her. And she gazed at the glass wall the way that same child might look out the kitchen window and see her friends out on the street playing in the fading sunlight before bedtime. The difference, Smitty noted, was that when the child eventually choked down the pale beans she would rise and join her playmates. At that moment, Smitty decided that he would do something special for the fish.

At the other end of the exhibit, Dr. Dorfman was arranging a fossil display of coelacanth specimens dating back through the years. Many he had unearthed himself back in New Jersey. For him, it was an unprecedented opportunity to present an actual living specimen in conjunction with the fossil record. And while Dorfman's fossil record was impressive, he would be the first to admit that it paled in comparison to the living incarnation swimming a few feet away.

When the scientist saw the handyman approach, he called out, "Smitty, you're an absolute artist! This is the nicest display I've ever worked with—custom cases, handmade coelacanth scales carved into the wood. They're magnificent! They don't even need fossils!"

Smitty grinned.

"Really," Dorfman continued, "you should be working for the Museum of Natural History."

Smitty replied graciously, "I think I'm where I'm supposed to be."

"Aren't we all?" Dorfman agreed.

"I have an idea for the coelacanth," he began.

Dorfman listened. He was a big fan of ideas, and had a few of his own. While everyone at SeaTopia believed that this would be the only canth in captivity, and were lobbying the authorities to issue them a permit to display their specimen in perpetuity, Dorfman saw things differently. Ever the man of science, he was prepared to argue that this canth should be the first of several held in captivity. Aside from the obvious display and study value, Dorfman believed that a breeding population could be created in captivity, resulting in live specimens in aquariums and universities all over the world, without ever taking additional creatures from the wild. Moreover, he argued that a breeding population in captivity would help ensure the survival of the wild breeds if some type of disease or environmental condition ever killed them off. They could be produced in captivity and then reintroduced in a suitable habitat. The same technique could be used to increase the animal's range even before any disaster decimated the canths. But there were many, Dave among them, who would take issue with the plan.

"I don't know canths like you do," Smitty continued, "but this one looks unhappy."

"Well," the ichthyologist nudged his glasses further up the bridge of his sun burnt nose, "if you don't know the animal, how can you tell it's unhappy?"

Dorfman waved over the very young man who was sent to SeaTopia in place of Helen Campbell. He was her assistant from Queensland who really did know his canths. At the moment, he was the only person in SeaTopia, perhaps even in the Americas, who had actually studied living coelacanths in their natural habitat, although his experience was only with the Indonesian population.

"Here comes the youngest *expert* I've ever seen," Dorfman quipped, "but the kid knows his stuff, no doubt about that." Then, raising his voice, he yelled, "Kemar, Smitty thinks the canth is unhappy. What do you think?"

Kemar slipped on a pair of beat-up wire-rimmed glasses from a small bag hanging off his belt. He kneeled down and pulled up a weighted line that was submerged in the tank. Three thermometers were tied to the line, each recording a different depth of the tank. "Temperatures look good," the expert observed.

"Could it be something else?" Smitty asked.

"Must be," Kemar continued. "Why do you think she's depressed, I mean other than the fact that she's in a tank?"

"That's not exactly a specimen jar," Dr. Dorfman pointed out.

"Would you like to spend your life in a tank?" Kemar asked.

"I'm not a coelacanth," Dorfman answered.

"What if you were?" Kemar pressed.

"If I was, we wouldn't be having this conversation."

"Look at her," Smitty uncharacteristically interrupted. "She's so sluggish, she's out of it—she doesn't seem right." Given the fact that no coelacanth had ever survived this long in captivity, there was enormous concern, spoken or not, that this canth could die before anyone really saw, studied or marketed it.

"Give her a chance to settle in. She hasn't been here all that long," Dorfman said. "We've seen it before. New fish enter the tank and take a little time to adjust. The water, her vitals, all the numbers are there. She just needs to come around mentally, to accept the situation."

Feeling more for the coelacanth with every word spoken, Kemar mumbled, "Perhaps she won't accept the situation."

"The coelacanth survival instinct must be pretty strong. She'll pull through. She'll adjust. Son, she has no choice," the scientist concluded.

Shaking his head, Kemar removed the glasses and dropped them back in the sack. "There's always a choice."

"That's what I'm talking about," Smitty added. "I've heard

how fragile these fish can be. What if she wills herself right out of here?"

"You mean dies?" Dorfman asked.

"That's exactly what I mean, or even just gets herself real sick. It could happen."

"So what's the answer? Any expert advice for us, Kemar?" The biologist was interested to see what the young man would suggest, but before he could say anything, Smitty began to tell a story.

"When I was a kid, I loved to eat. I looked forward to every meal and never missed one. I went to stay at my cousin's house for the summer. I was very excited. He lived in Baton Rouge. I figured there'd be all kinds of great food, Creole dishes and stuff like that. My mouth was dripping before I even got off the train. But when I finally got there, almost everything my aunt fed us came from a can. We didn't have fresh vegetables or a home-cooked meal, not a single crawfish, the entire summer."

"So you want to cook for the canth?" Dorfman asked.

"You're missing my point. Other than the food, I had a blast. We went to the movies. We went swimming. We had adventures. It was great, but when I returned home and my parents asked me how it went, I said, 'Don't ever send me back there.' And the only reason I said that was because of the food."

"But you still had your good time and you survived," the elder biologist pointed out.

"But in the end, I was miserable, and I knew I was going home in a few weeks. If I thought I was stayin' forever, eating canned creamed corn, who knows how depressed I'd have gotten."

Dorfman smiled. It was tough to tell whether he was amused with the story or thought that its suggestions were absurd. Either way, he smiled.

Kemar pursued the implication of Smitty's analogy. "So you think this canth needs a better diet? Do you know what she eats?"

"No, I don't pretend to know much of anything. That's where you guys come in. Whatever she eats, maybe you can give it to her alive. I mean, she's eating that same lifeless crap, frozen or canned, that I had to endure. If you tossed her some live food, she'd have to be more active just to catch it."

"Live lantern fish," Dorfman contemplated as he scratched his chin. "Tough to get... not as clean as frozen... I'd hate to see her get sick from that."

"Maybe she's already sick," Kemar suggested. He picked up a half thawed mullet and bounced it in his palm. "If she's like her cousins in Indonesia, she might eat squid, eels, cardinal fish. I've seen canths eat octopus..."

Samantha knew she wasn't supposed to be in the exhibit. She knew it wasn't opened to the general public, but reasoned, conveniently, that she was no longer part of the general public. She was now an employee of SeaTopia, and had the shirt and shorts to prove it. This gave her certain rights and privileges. However, deep down she knew that sneaking into the coelacanth exhibit was not one of those rights. But she also knew that she was going in anyway.

Samantha tucked her staff shirt into her staff shorts and straightened her name-tag. Everyone who worked at SeaTopia wore a name-tag. The names were all fish inspired monikers derived from the employee's given name. The woman who sold the tickets was Jilly-fish. The man who flipped burgers was Barry-cuda. The fellow who stocked shelves in the gift shop was Sea-Horace. The tag pinned to Samantha's shirt read, 'Samantha-ray'. Gone were the days of Shortstripe. Samantha-ray tucked in her shirt, straightened her tag and strode right into the exhibit. When she came to the "CLOSED" sign, a grasshopper jumping across the floor caused her to look down. She could honestly say, well almost, that she did not see the sign. When she approached one saying "DO NOT ENTER," Samantha dropped her pen.

Again, she missed the sign. As she encountered the "AUTHORIZED PERSONNEL ONLY" sign, sawdust somehow flew into her eyes. She shut them tightly just as she passed the warning, missing the sign. But when she saw an older man staining a flat wooden coelacanth laid across two saw horses, Samantha decided that she needed a more sophisticated plan.

The man looked up from his project. He stared at the girl for a moment, as if he was waiting for a hall pass or some type of password. Samantha returned the stare, confident on the outside, but panicked on the inside. And then it came to her, the perfect plan… foolproof. She pulled out her tattered notebook and gave the Flipper journal an official looking tap. Obviously, she had important business inside. Smitty nodded and returned to staining his wooden coelacanth.

Samantha stepped into the exhibit and immediately looked around to see if she was alone. Reckoning she was, and hoping no one else would come in, she studied the tank. It was different from any other in the park; different from anything she'd ever seen. The canth's tank was a tall cylinder. Viewing could take place from above, outdoors, where Samantha now stood. But all she could see was the sun reflect off the windblown water with a deep dark patch beneath. She leaned over the rail, careful not to re-enact her performance at the dolphin tank, and peered into the deep. She saw nothing.

She realized that the best viewing would be from below, where there were two floors of full length glass. She had heard that the rear of its cave was also finished in glass, so the canth would never be out of the viewing public's sight. The canth was far too special, and expensive, a guest to allow for moments when it couldn't be viewed, especially when patrons would pay a separate admission to see Maputa.

Samantha spotted a helpful photographic display that explained the tank. On the bottom level, more glass panels circled the tank. When the fish came out to feed, people would be able to see it interact with an unnatural imitation of its natural habitat. Again, the illusion worked better for the humans than the coelacanth. One look and Samantha knew just whom this tank was really for. User friendly applied to those living outside, not to the one living inside.

As proud as she was of her new affiliation with SeaTopia, Samantha shuddered when she spotted the display above the stairwell that led to the lower levels of the tank. The coelacanth had a corporate sponsor, a plastic bag company. The huge sign read, "When SeaTopia needed to Seal-a-canth, they called us." The ad implied that SeaTopia called "Eco-Plast" for expert advice on how to construct such a wonderful tank, which of course wasn't true. The only green motivation Eco-Plast understood grew in a cash register. In fact, the only expertise Eco-Plast shared with SeaTopia was their skill at writing a check and attaching their name to the enormous publicity the dino-fish would generate. They were presently lobbying to name the poor creature Seal and copyright its image for packaging and promotion. There was talk about cookie-canth lunchbox treats and crispie-canth cereal shaped like its distinctive scales. But Samantha and Maputa knew none of this. Another person who knew none of this, whose mind could not comprehend the commercialization and exploitation of nature solely for profit's sake, entered the exhibit just as Samantha reached down and turned the knob on the door that said, "Stairway to levels A & B." A second sign taped to the door warned, "Entrance Forbidden." Samantha missed that one. When it came to reading signs, Samantha was the poster-child for selective attention.

Jiggling the knob a second time, Samantha heard, "Can I help you with something?"

A word she often heard in her mother's condo complex came to mind. *Busted.* She froze, afraid to turn and face the voice.

"Are you looking for me?" the person inquired.

Samantha shook her head from side to side, hand stuck to the door knob, hoping whoever it was would leave.

This time it spoke more quietly. "You want to see her, don't you?"

Again Samantha moved her head, this time nodding up and down, her hand still attached to the incriminating knob. It was no doubt the single biggest piece of damning evidence, yet for some unknown reason she clung to it like a lifeline. If she released it, she might tumble into nothingness, or worse, lose her job, her SeaTopia staff shirt and be escorted from the park, "asked" never to return. Why had she been so stupid? In two weeks' time she would've been able to see the canth to her heart's content. If the voice belonged to someone higher on the SeaTopia food chain than her, which wasn't difficult for her to imagine, she might not see the canth, now or ever.

There was, however, a friendly quality, a hint of amusement pulsing through the timbre of the voice. When one spoke as infrequently as Samantha, one often heard things in words that others ignored. Samantha had a quiet tongue, but a practiced ear.

The source of the voice stepped closer. A hand appeared next to Samantha's. "It's okay, I understand curiosity. Would you like to come down with me and see her?" The hand had a key in it. Samantha released the knob. The key entered the lock and the door opened.

The stairwell was dark, not yet lit for the public. Samantha could not tell who was with her. She had not yet faced the face. It did not sound like the man who sanded the wooden coelacanth. It did not sound like Dave either.

"Let's look in at Level B. I'll bet anything she's in her cave. You can get a good look at her." Another door swung open. But when they stepped into the florescent light of Level B, Samantha didn't know what surprised her more, the awesome sight of the dino-fish in the cave, or the unexpected presence of a boy not much older than her with keys to the exhibit, checking temperatures, salinity, oxygen, pressures and charts as if he were some type of scientist.

He turned, smiled and said, "Amazing, isn't she?"

Samantha nodded. She approached the glass, opened her fingers wide and laid them on the cold pane. A second later, her forehead rested on the glass as well. Maputa drew the girl toward the tank. Samantha was blown away by the sight of a creature she had never seen before: alive, huge and inches from her.

Reading her name backwards off the glass, the boy scientist said, "So you are Samantha-ray. I had a friend named Son Ba, but I've never known a Samantha... My name is Kemar." And since the girl seemed to have nothing to say, he continued, "I can't quite figure out what's wrong with the canth."

When she heard the phrase, "wrong with the canth" Samantha turned to Kemar and faced him, looking quite concerned.

"Oh yes, something's wrong. Nothing shown in any of these charts or indicators, but something's not right. She could be eating more—should be, actually. She's sluggish. She's not right." Although he spoke to her, his thoughts were completely with the canth.

"She's in a tank," Samantha whispered, as if by whispering, she wasn't actually speaking.

Kemar grinned, "I knew I was missing something." He thought for a moment, looked around furtively and whispered, "Here's what we'll do. We'll take her out, put her on a gurney and slip her into the surf. That should make her feel better."

The girl nodded, leaned closer and replied, "Not now, there's someone up there. How will we—"

Kemar waved at her, trying to get her attention, "Hey, maybe there's a less drastic answer? A simple food supplement might change everything. Do you really think we should just toss her back in the—" Suddenly Kemar was reminded of his friend Al, whom he had met on Makoona. His thoughts drifted back to a moment when Al, a fisherman, returned a rare stargazer to the reef solely because it was rare. Al had recorded some information and then threw it back. Had he thought about it longer, Kemar would have been forced to ask himself why it was okay to remove this fish, yet still believe that other endangered creatures should remain in their natural habitats. The answer was not simple.

But Kemar's ruminations were ruined when Samantha stated simply, "She doesn't want to be here."

Directing his internal question toward Samantha, Kemar asked, "So you think the canth should leave, or perhaps all of these creatures should be returned?"

She smiled, raised her eyebrows and said nothing.

Kemar pinched the bridge of his nose with his thumb and index finger. He spread them apart, above his eyes, massaging his forehead and temples. Speaking to himself as much as to Samantha, he said, "This is a strange place to work if you believe that these animals belong in the ocean."

Again, the girl smiled and shrugged. She was pretty sure that she liked Kemar. She suspected that he, like the creatures around him, would have been more at home on the open sea than in a tank. Samantha sat on the floor across from Maputa. She opened her notebook, stared into the canth's cave, and began to write. Kemar noticed, but did not question. He had his own business to attend to.

Inside the tank, Shareef grew restless. He had examined every inch of their new home. As the days had dragged into weeks, the shrimp's adventure became less adventurous, so he decided to take matters into his own fore-claws. He landed on Maputa's face. A large eye lowered and looked. "Yes, Shareef?" the canth cooed.

"Don't want to create any turbulence, I know how you worry about me, but I'm planning a bit of a trip."

"Really... and where will you be going?" Maputa asked without interest. "To the rock over there, perhaps? Under the sand down there? Up to the surface for a little sun?" The canth did not like the sun or the surface. Maputa grinned and added, "Have a nice trip. I'm sure we'll be drifting into each other again real soon." The massive fish, confident that Shareef was going nowhere, returned to thoughts of better days in bluer water.

The shrimp nodded and began his journey. Not at all sure *where* he was going, he was sure *that* he was going. The shrimp slid behind a rock at the base of the cave. Directly above it, at the very top of the tank, clean salt water cascaded onto the rocks. But where Shareef stood on his trusty jointed legs, water was being sucked into a black hole. A hard covering, gray like the rocks, guarded the hole. Louvered slits prevented large particles, like stones and coelacanths, from passing through, into whatever waited beyond. But Shareef was no large particle. And this was one of those times when being less was actually more. The shrimp let the current pull him into the slotted opening. He held his carapace and abdomen flat across the gill-like covering, took a few deep breaths of water and then allowed himself to be sucked into the dark hole. The shrimp disappeared.

Shareef lost his bearings immediately. There was no light and the current was strong. He could only surrender to it and try to steady himself, literally "going with the flow." A low moan followed him along the way. It was not his own. It reminded him of the sound that came from the floating islands of the man-tide. Shareef began to wonder whether leaving the safety of the tank was such a good idea, but he felt deep within his carapace that leaving the confines of the tank was a good idea, no matter how this ended.

Just as he came to that conclusion, the shrimp was slammed into a hard tight mesh. He still couldn't see, but he could feel the water passing through all around him. The current held him, yet Shareef was not pinned. He could move, somewhat, his fore-claws, the second set of pincers behind them and the three pairs of legs behind them. He dragged himself across the mesh. There were pieces of dirt, remnants of plant life, waste, organic matter and other impurities that were welcome neither in gill nor sea.

The water surrounding the mesh, even though it flowed, irritated the shrimp's gill rakers as he breathed in the refuse. His concentration slipped, and so did he as he tried to move against the suction on the slippery screen. Shareef climbed over a dead leech, its body drawn halfway through, clogging several holes in the mesh, other debris building up around it as the refuse floated in.

The shrimp continued to explore the obstruction. He had no choice. Swimming back the way he came was not an option. Resting, he surrendered to the current, letting the force of it hold him in place against the mesh. Then he saw something, a glimmer. Lines of wavy illumination bounced in the distance. A second path was also feeding into the mesh. The shrimp wondered where it led. He gazed at the glimmer that seemed to be his only hope.

The current that came from it was just as strong as the one that carried him originally, but there was something different about this path. It was shorter... and dirtier. The tunnel that came from the glimmer had lumps and clumps of plaque and sludge all along its walls. He could not swim there, but he might be able to crawl.

The shrimp climbed down the mesh to the lowest part of the tunnel; sunk his pointed, jointed legs into the muck and tried to step towards the light at the end of the tunnel. If he angled his legs properly, the current actually pushed them deeper into the debris, giving him better traction.

Shareef laid his antennae back against his body to reduce resistance. He hid behind the taller mounds of sludge, using them to obstruct the current. Slowly, he made his way to the light. It could be done. He could make it, unless, of course, he lost his footing. Then the current would instantly sweep him up and carry him back to the mesh. This would happen every time he slipped.

"Had the dead leech tried the same plan?" Shareef wondered. In order to reach the light, like a hatchling turtle heading to the sea, he would need a flawless crawl. Other problems would only be an issue if Shareef made it to the light. What would be waiting for him when he emerged from the tunnel? And where would he be?

The shrimp smiled to himself, thinking, "If there's a lonely coelacanth on the other side of that light, I'm gonna be one crabby crustacean."

Gilgongo had recovered nicely from his wounds. He had gotten so used to his prosthetic flipper that he felt healed. The turtle swam around his tank enjoying the vacation, the luxury and the company of the manatee. At times the sun was a bit too bright, the diet a bit too limited. And lately, the turtle wondered how long it would be before he returned to the sea. Still, he was having a nice time in the tank next to Naillij.

Again the turtle remembered the injured bird named Lupé who couldn't fly and shared a large patch of seaweed with Gilgongo's family while he recovered. Eventually, with some help from the turtles' mother, Pingolo, Lupé became strong enough to fly. The petrel popped into the air and flew off. Gilgongo wondered whether the bird ever found the islands or the mate he searched for. The turtle wondered whether his own journey would continue, or had it ended?

The manatee who listened to Gilgongo pointed out, "Ah, but it's not fair to look at this moment as an end. Surely you would've perished in the dunes, and surely your journey would've ceased before you ever arrived here. The same is true for me. Perhaps we're both living from this moment on, on borrowed time."

"Maybe… but what does that mean? Do we live differently on 'borrowed time' and who have we borrowed it from?"

"I don't know," the manatee replied. "I don't believe the man-tide has given us this time, since they're really the reason why we were in trouble in the first place... And if we've borrowed this time, it implies that we will have to pay it back at some point. I'm not sure I believe that either."

"The time we have now might be a gift, not borrowed at all," Gilgongo suggested.

"But again, a gift from whom?"

"It is a very confusing situation that we are in. There are plenty of questions and very few answers." It was a thought all the creatures of SeaTopia, even some of the man-tide, would have agreed on.

The manatee returned to the conversation. "You know, had you been left on those dunes, you would have found the answer to all this."

"Yes," Gilgongo agreed, "whether we're in that water," he nodded toward the ocean, "or in this water, we will all find the answer one day."

"What would you do if you were suddenly free, out of here?" Naillij asked.

"Are you kidding?"

"What would you do? Give me a breaker, indulge me," the manatee teased.

"Okay. I'd eat a few jellyfish, right away. Then a couple sponges. Then, I'd get a cleaning, not just any cleaning, a good goby cleaning—from beak to bottom, flipper to fin. Ooh, I miss that."

The two friends lifted their heads above the wall of the tank. They looked out over the grounds of SeaTopia and then to the beach beyond. Both took a deep breath of cool wet air, slid back into the water and swam to the gate that separated the two tanks. The turtle and the manatee faced each other. Naillij nudged the mesh that filled the gate. It was the closest she could get to nuzzling her friend.

Gilgongo returned the gesture with a soft swipe of his fore-fin. He turned to swim a lazy circle and brushed the mesh with his one healthy hind flipper. The flipper stuck to the gate. The turtle tugged, but he was not released. He stretched his neck, straining to see what was happening. Although he had recently taken a good breath, he was caught underwater and could not break the surface with his head. If he could not free himself, he would drown.

The manatee appeared on the other side of the gate. A tag that the man-tide had snapped onto Gilgongo's flipper had snagged the mesh. Not nearly as alarmed as the turtle, Naillij said, "You're the only animal I know who gets caught *after* it's already been caught."

The turtle was in no mood for marine mammal witticisms. He tugged on the tag, trying to free himself.

"Relax," Naillij warned. "You're going to make it tougher to get you out of this." The manatee tried to chew through the mesh, but quickly saw that the teeth of an aquatic grazer would not suffice. Gilgongo's beak might've been up to the task, but he could not contort himself into position.

The manatee was becoming concerned for her friend when a hand broke through the surface and gently nudged her from the gate. The hand reached deeper, pinched the tag, and popped it from the mesh. The hand held the turtle until another entered the water. The second hand held a fairly large metal claw that clamped over the tag, pressing it down tighter against the skin of the fin. The other hand released the turtle and Gilgongo swam off with a reassuring caress along the top of his shell. The hands disappeared from the water. A few moments later, several strips of squid landed in Gilgongo's tank, followed by the splash of several lettuce heads on the manatee's side.

Dave dropped the pliers into a rusty red tool box. He turned to Smitty and said, "Thanks."

"Always happy to help." The handyman drove off to his next project in his green golf cart. Smitty amused himself with the thought that most men his age who retired to Florida used their golf carts to get to the next hole. The next hole that Smitty's cart carried him to usually required putty rather than a putter.

Dave glanced back at the tank, a figure eight joined in the middle with the gate. He was happy that both the manatee and the turtle had been saved. It was one of the most satisfying moments that his job had to offer, the fact that he could atone for some of the damage usually caused by his fellow humans.

But saving these creatures begged another difficult question. Should they remain in SeaTopia, or should they return to the sea? Dave looked up from the rehab tank, shifting his gaze east, to the ocean. Legally, he could keep both animals in the aquarium for the rest of their lives. Even though they were protected species, SeaTopia had a license to treat, display and hold these creatures. Dave wrestled with a conundrum that never went away, even after he had answered it thousands of times. Should all these wonderful creatures be returned to the sea, or should some of them serve as ambassadors, building awareness and affection for their cousins who roamed free out there, somewhere?

Deciding that he would not suddenly be able to answer the question, Dave tossed a few more squid and another head of lettuce into the tank.

On the walk back to his office, Dave considered the manatee. He tried to convince himself that since she would have died out there had he not saved her, that perhaps she owed her new life, her re-birth, to playing a role at SeaTopia. In some small way, her presence might generate more funds for the aquarium, permitting Dave and his staff to save other animals.

But Dave also knew that her injuries were caused by the hull and prop of someone's boat. He knew that the turtle's flipper was destroyed because of a person's careless use of fishing line. And so, really, while he had saved the animals, in some way he had also caused their pain. And while they were alive and well, they had lost a part of themselves. *They* certainly owed *him* nothing.

There were, however, debts that Dave was not so good at paying, not so quick to accept. SeaTopia, after all, was a business. Dave was expected to make a profit as he kept not only the fish, but the coffers healthy too. Generally speaking, the former was significantly healthier than the latter.

Dave resisted animal shows. In the past, the park had pilot whales, penguins, otters, petting tanks and other types of entertaining fluff. As the director of SeaTopia, he believed that education, not entertainment was the mandate and that they weren't mutually exclusive.

One thought that kept him smiling, that kept him focused and energized, was the belief that if a park like SeaTopia was going to exist, the animals would be better served, whether they realized it or not, by someone who truly loved them than by someone more interested in marketing them.

He did, however, have the dolphins do a pair of shows daily, but he thought they seemed to enjoy the activity. They were so smart and energetic; he felt that the performances actually made their captivity more bearable. There was also a sting-ray feeding tank; less stressful than petting and the rays got paid in food, which the patrons purchased from the park. But this was about as far as Dave was willing to go. He was not an organ grinder and these were not his, or anyone's monkeys.

The Director had also shunned exotics, not caring for the way many of these fish were captured. However, it was not lost on him that the canth was probably the most exotic fish in captivity anywhere on the planet. Dave tried to stress local species. There were certainly plenty of them and they were every bit as interesting as any other fish. These were the creatures most of the patrons would encounter in their daily lives. It all made sense to Dave, but it didn't necessarily create the longest lines at the ticket booths, allowing Jilly-fish plenty of time, on the clock, to do her nails each day.

The one commercial concession Dave had made, at the

urging of the board, was to accept the coelacanth. The canth would be a fiscal home-run, but Dave felt somewhat Faustian, as if he had sold his soul to the devil. In one fish, in one specimen, he had compromised almost all of the principles he fought for on a daily basis. The coelacanth was undoubtedly an exotic, rare and an enormous attraction. Dave hoped that the sheer educational value of the creature would somehow justify the personal betrayals. He also prayed, that in the end, this canth would have helped protect the rest of her kind and generate a better quality of life for every other creature at the aquarium.

Lastly, he prayed that this incredible animal, like all the others in SeaTopia, would forgive him.

Cariam explored every inch of the tank that he could reach. He had mentally mapped every nook and cranny of both the ocean tank and the reef tank. He had even visited a third tank that contained a collection of rays. While both the octopus and the gazer had decided that the unpredictable, volatile nature of Quala, the shark tank, was something they would avoid, Cariam knew he might have to return there if all went according to plan.

For the moment, the two friends took solace in the living coral where they were free to behave in whatever manner suited them, where they didn't have to practice covering each other's fins. They were still careful, however; the coral, sand and walls had ears, even in the friendly tank. Scorpion-fish, soles and others could hide themselves and listen in. Words had a way of drifting into other tanks, washing across other fish.

The octopus and the gazer did what they were best equipped to do. Cariam turned a pale blue with sandy flecks, flattened himself out and perched in a crevice where the wall joined the sand. Norton buried himself next to his friend. They disappeared and whispered.

"I think I can get out of here," the octopus began.

"You think we can get out of here?" Norton echoed.

"Not exactly... I think I can. I haven't figured out your escape."

"Would you go without me?"

"Would you want me to stay if I could go?"

The gazer shook his head, but his disappointment could be seen in the two small eyes that peered above the surface of the sand.

"Look Norton, if I don't think about getting out of here, I'm gonna go crazy. I don't intend to wind up like them." The octopus pointed in five different directions to indicate drone-like fish who circled the tank all day, every day. While they resembled fish physically, they no longer behaved like creatures of the sea.

"I have to at least plan," Cariam continued. "Whether I do it or not isn't important now. Help me with this. It'll be good for us... and I might even be able to figure something out for you."

"You think?" Norton asked hopefully.

"I don't know. Let's try."

Norton agreed. They would try to find a way out.

"We have one thing going for us," Cariam began. "The ocean is right out there. I've seen it."

"Yeah, but what ocean? It doesn't look like Peace to me." The gazer referred to the Ocean of Peace, where he and Cariam hailed from.

"Fishionally, I don't care what ocean it is. It has no walls."

Norton nodded. "I could talk to some of the fish in here... ask them what they know about the water out there. Some of them are locals. I bet they could tell us a lot."

The octopus interrupted, "They might even know how to get to Peace..."

The gazer smiled beneath a veil of sand. "You don't need them for that. I can tell you."

"But you said you don't know where we are? You don't know the ocean out there."

"I don't know the ocean out there, but I think I would know

how to find Peace."

Cariam looked confused. He even flashed a puzzled purple, revealing himself for an instant.

"I'm a stargazer, remember? I might not have the brain of an octopus, but you get me out there under the open sky, and if there aren't too many clouds, I'll know how to get home. The stars don't lie and I know how to read them."

"Well, now I can't leave without you," the octopus laughed.

Norton hoped his friend was telling him the truth.

One thing is certain for a fish living in a tank: If they manage to get alone, they won't be alone for long. The angel, Pagre, drifted a few fins from the two friends. Either he didn't see them, or he was so occupied with his own thoughts that he ignored them. Perhaps he noticed the conversation and was merely being polite. The angel rummaged through some rubble, in search of a rouge morsel that drifted to the bottom unnoticed by the other fish. On rare occasions, he'd locate some appetizing algae, a treat among treats. Algae were as rare as lobster scales, but Pagre had a nose for finding it.

Norton and Cariam didn't really know what to make of the angelfish. While some seemed to think that he was connected to the spirit fish, as the sole had told them, others disregarded the thought. Many of them believed that the angelfish was just another casualty of captivity, not unlike those fish on Makoona who became a little crazy after being sprayed by man-tide cyanide fishers.

In the predator tank, Pagre was held up as an example of what could happen to fish who clung to the past, who believed in something that couldn't be true. After all, if there was a spirit, would it allow something like this to happen? Cariam and Norton preferred not to dwell on the "why" or the "how" of their situation. It did nothing to improve the reality of the moment.

The two watched Pagre pick at the scraps under the rocks. Quietly powerful, the angelfish moved the rocks aside with a unique blend of strength and grace. He would ingest a morsel, savor it for a second and then get back to work. There was a rhythm to his movements, a meditation. The fish was doing more than eating, more than scavenging. He refused to stop being who he was.

Pagre was the only fish in any of the tanks who did not swim to the surface when feeding time came. He did not eat the food that was still frozen, that still had the unpleasant scent of fingers on it. And while one would assume that by passing up the easy pickings at feeding time Pagre would go hungry, he did not. In fact, the angel was as stout and as thick as any of his kind should be. Because others had given up on scavenging, on being who they really were, Pagre found plenty of food. Perhaps some food even found him.

The angelfish seemed to be remarkably true to himself. As a result, he appeared to be relatively unaffected by his captivity, although no one really knew what was going on deep beneath his scales. On the surface, at least, Pagre looked to be calm, even and generally content.

Norton pointed out to Cariam that he sensed that Pagre was waiting for something, as if he expected the man-tide to reach into the tank, pick him up and drop him back into the sea. The two friends found the behavior fascfinating, but rejected it for themselves. They could not accept the idea that they were suddenly going to be released. They chose a more pro-active solution, not suspecting just how pro-active the hungry angel actually was.

Cariam wondered whether they should share their plans with the angelfish. Maybe what he was really waiting for were two fish like them, two fish with a plan, even if they didn't quite have the plan part yet. They did like Pagre. He certainly seemed like he wouldn't demand to come along. But could he keep a secret? The octopus and the gazer sat silently, waiting for the angelfish to move on.

Pagre, however, had his own plans. He continued to feed, getting closer and closer to the gazer and the octopus. When he was virtually on top of Norton, turning over rocks all around the gazer, the fish rose up and greeted the angel. "How is the food today, Pagre?"

Not at all surprised by the appearance of Norton, the angel answered, "How could food be anything but good? Care to join me? Tell Cariam he's welcome too. No need to hide from me, unless you're a scrap, of course." The angel turned to where the octopus had cloaked himself and said to the lump of blue coral, "Come, join us... plenty for everyone."

Outed by the angel, Cariam turned from blue to brown and jetted himself closer with a pinch of his siphon. Pagre continued, "No need to be afraid of me. I'm not an Angel, I'm an angelfish."

"Well, *we've* heard you're a fish, who's an Angel," Norton explained.

"Even if that were true, why would you fear me? Fishionally, I'd love to be friends with an Angel. Wouldn't that be wet?"

"But you must admit," the octopus probed, "it would be a little strange."

"Why?"

"I don't know... I mean, the Spirit is something out there. It's not really something that's right next to you, something that an octopus eats a meal and chats with."

"Seems to me, that's *exactly* what the Spirit is. What do you think, Norton?"

"Well, Cariam's a great friend, but he's not much of a Fishtian, not that I am either, but I think the Spirit is a lot closer than we realize. Sometimes, when I'm buried in a sandy flat, daytime or nighttime, I know I'm not alone. And I'm not talking about some leech or worm sharing the hole with me, I know there's this presence." Norton stopped, looked at the other two, wondering whether to continue, and said, "You know, I talk to the presence... not out loud. I wouldn't catch much if I did, but inside myself. I do it all the time. It makes me feel good and helps me figure things out. I'm thinking it might be the Spirit."

Pagre swam over to Norton and whispered, "Of course it is. Your friend out there has not forgotten you. Blessed are those who have not seen and yet believe."

Cariam interrupted, "I gotta tell ya, I'm having a little trouble with this. If Norton speaks to the Spirit and you're supposed to be an Angel, then what the fin are we doing in here?"

"You think because Seaqoyit sees you, your life is supposed to be perfect?"

"This is pretty far from perfect."

"Actually, it's pretty close to perfect." Pagre was enjoying the chat.

The octopus turned red. "Dead coral, walls, frozen food. Not another octopus anywhere in sight? This is close to perfect?"

"Well, what's perfect, Cariam? You tell me."

The octopus considered the request. He furrowed his mantle, raised three arms, pointed to the ocean and said, "Out there, that's perfect."

Pagre nodded his agreement. "Yes. It is the Spirit's perfection... Can you see it?"

Now Norton nodded.

"Can you smell it, taste it, feel it? Then it would seem to me that you are, indeed, *close* to perfection."

"You say I'm close. I say I'm a world away."

"Then let the Spirit be the current that carries you home, to perfection, to Peace."

"Anytime the Spirit wants to do that, I'm ready," Cariam declared. "In the meantime, I think I'm gonna use some of my Spirit given abilities to find my own way out of here. Right Norton?"

The gazer did not speak.

"Nothing much around here to be thankful for," Cariam

mumbled.

"You have nothing to be thankful for?" Pagre pursued.

The octopus did not answer.

"Well, if you truly believe that, throw yourself from this tank. Climb out of the water and perish in the sun. Die in the waterless air. If your breath and your life mean nothing, then do that. Go ahead. I'll help you. Why have you not moved? Go, breach on the beach." The angelfish waited a moment, then smiled brightly. He touched Cariam with his fin and whispered into his mantle, "You see, your life does have meaning. Your existence does have value. Your future does have hope. Even in here, you are blessed."

"Do you really believe that? Look at where we are," Cariam countered.

"I prefer to look at what we are, but let's answer your question. 'Where are we?' We are in the very same place. We breathe the very same water. Yet you are miserable, unhappy. While I feel joy, see beauty and look forward to tomorrow. So who is better off?"

"But when it's all said and done, where will you be and what will you have? I'll tell you, you'll be in a tank and you'll have nothing."

"Where will you be?" Pagre pressed. "I am a fishtian, a son of Seaqoyit. It can never be taken from me. I am not afraid. I will be with the spirit wearing scales of glory. And I'll let you in on a little secret: I'm already there."

"Forgive me, Pagre, but I know where you are. I see the truth," the octopus said.

Pagre grinned, "Good, because the truth will set you free."

"Sprayed, definitely sprayed," Cariam concluded.

"Perhaps if you listened to the voice, the Spirit, your voice would be louder and the Spirit would hear you."

"Well, what does that mean?"

"How can you be surprised that a god, who deep down you

don't have faith in, has not granted you your request? First, you must believe. It's easy to love Seaqoyit when all is going well, but if you can love the spirit, here, now, then the love is real."

"But how real can Seaqoyit's love, or Seaqoyit himself be, if we're subjected to this? It makes no sense to me."

"It always comes back to that, doesn't it? Well, Seaqoyit doesn't serve me, I serve the spirit. And so, I'm happy here, because this is where the spirit has placed me. I don't know why, but I don't need to know. I am the servant, not the master."

"Yes, you are," the octopus agreed. "A foolfish servant, I dare say."

"Cariam!" Norton protested.

"No, really," the octopus reiterated.

"We are all fools," Pagre said softly. "You accuse me of being a fool for the spirit? I plead guilty... Let me ask you, does the sun rise before it sets or set before it has risen? For me, the sun has risen and it will never set... This tank is the ultimate temptation to abandon my belief. But my faith is stronger than all this, much stronger."

"Yet you do nothing. Is that faith?" the octopus probed.

Pagre opened his gills and took a deep breath before he spoke. "Sometimes we're called upon to do more than we feel we're capable of. The most devout are often prepared to accept that, but sometimes the spirit asks us to do *less*. And that's what many aren't ready for. You're ready to fight your way out of here. That's brave and noble, but perhaps the spirit is calling on you to wait, to avoid the battle outside the tank and suffer through the one inside. That might actually be a more benthic sacrifice than taking the action you yearn for. So be careful, sometimes the spirit will ask us to do *less* than we want to. Me, I will bear this shell. It's what I've been called to do. Want to know what you can do?"

"Go ahead, Pagre. I had a feeling you wanted something."

"Oh, not just me. I've heard that there's a very special fish, alone in a tank, half alive, half dead. Would you go to her, before you escape, and tell her that she is not forgotten, that she will be saved?" Pagre stared into the face of the octopus, beyond the mollusk's eyes and the shifting colors of his flesh. This was a question asked of the soul.

Cariam contemplated the bizarre request.

"I will do it," his friend the gazer declared. "I will tell her, myself."

Pagre hugged the gazer with his short fins. "I love this fish. Here is your perfection. It couldn't be any closer. Thank you, Norton, but this is not your shell to bear."

"And why isn't it yours?" the octopus challenged.

"Because I have not been blessed with the means, and I have not been asked. Will *you* do it?"

Cariam thought it over. There was something about the phrase, "not your shell to bear" that grabbed hold of him. Back on Makoona, he had heard rumors about his mother, Binti, that she was obsessed with finding a shell because as an octopus, she was a mollusk without a shell. The irony had never plagued Cariam, but now, at this moment after hearing those words, it took hold. Was his mother's "shell" not a shell after all, but a holy mission, a divine deed? Was it being passed on to her son?

This time Norton spoke to his friend. "I can wait to escape. Will you bring hope to another whom you have never met, but needs you just the same? It is a worthy quest. Perhaps it is the reason you are here."

Cariam returned to the moment. He shook his head slowly, "We are here because we are forgotten, because we are on our own."

"You couldn't be more wrong, my friend." The angel spoke softly, yet with passion, "The spirit has heard the cry of your hearts, all three of them. The spirit knows every fish in the sea, every crab on the beach and every scale on the skin of every creature in the tanks." Pagre plucked a shiny yellow scale from his side and presented it to Cariam. "Deliver this to the canth. When you're believing, you'll be leaving."

"You might, but I won't be here. The voice I hear is telling me to leave." Cariam jetted himself to the tunnel that connected the reef fish with the predators and squeezed inside the tube leading to Quala.

Maputa had left SeaTopia. Her mind functioned, but her consciousness was suspended, muted. She placed herself somewhere else, using her surroundings to create an illusion, just as the man-tide hoped it would work for the visitors. She would emerge from her cave and hover in the water of the tank. Assuming the position of feeding and prayer, she did neither.

Maputa went coelatonic, dreaming her way home, back to her sheaf. She tried to retrieve moments in her life that she had already lived. Sometimes she would recreate moments exactly as they once happened, other times she'd alter a response or action and create new memories that weren't quite real.

But Maputa didn't concern herself with whether or not her memories were real. There was no law, no ethic that demanded she face the reality of her situation. The coelacanth would deal with SeaTopia on her own terms. Her thoughts were the one thing the man-tide could not control.

Maputa ate almost nothing. She choked down a scrap here and there to keep her heart beating and her gills breathing. She had the ability, although the man-tide was unaware, to slow her metabolism down to a point just above dormancy. Maputa allowed herself a thin fiber of hope anchored deep inside her mind. She did not recognize it. She did not think about it, but she would not permit the shard of hope to drift away.

Though she was physically alive, Maputa was not healthy. Being so close to death somehow made her visions more vivid. At times, the canth could not decide which was real, the vision or the tank. Perhaps she had been attacked by a Great White and was laying unconscious on the bottom of the sea, imagining all of this. Maybe she had died in the box with the lantern fish and was entombed in the mesh, buried at the bottom of the sea. Nilmah, Mombassa and her children might be circling around her, trying to wake her up. But no matter where her mind took her, eventually she returned to the tank. In the end, it was inescapable.

While Maputa chose to leave in her mind, Shareef left physically. At the moment, he felt that the canth had made a better choice. Covered in mud, his thorax rubbed the bottom as the shrimp crawled onward. Every step brought him that much closer to the bending light that bounced before him. Patient, determined, relentless; Shareef came within steps of the light.

Two things became clear. The light was not actually in the tunnel. It was in what looked to be a tank, much brighter than the one he had left. And, in order to reach it, another mesh would have to be crossed. Shareef wedged himself into the mesh. Resting, he watched, wondering if he should enter the tank.

As he waited, the rushing water washed the sludge from his body. He regained his translucent luster and confidence in his camouflage. The little shrimp with the big heart poked through a hole, released his grip on the mesh, swam clear of the current and entered the tank.

It was not only brighter, but bigger than the one he had left Maputa in. And there were many more residents. Shareef was fairly certain that he couldn't be seen beneath the white stone he crawled under. But there were many fish in the sea who could find their prey without ever seeing it. That worried Shareef. He had never seen many of the fish that swam among the rocks and coral. He didn't know what their abilities, or their tastes, might be. Still, it was exciting. It reminded him of what it was like to be back in the sea.

Shareef was ready to move. The path in front of him appeared clear. He would make a dash for what looked like a crop of hidden cup coral, yellow and brown. Its polyps seemed almost sick, different than the type he encountered in the wild. But that's what was in the tank, so that's where he would hide. The shrimp gathered himself, leaned into launching position, and then the sheltering stone disappeared. It was gone. He was exposed.

In an instant, Shareef was upside down. The light was gone. He was in a mouth, about to be swallowed. The shrimp did the only thing he could think of. He had seen fish with impressive dorsal spines who would drive them into the mouths of fish that swallowed them, forcing the predator to eject its prey. Although the spirit had not provided the shrimp with defensive spikes, Shareef was intelligent enough to apply the principle. He attacked the softest part of the predator's mouth; grabbing at flesh with his pincers, ripping, tearing, twisting. Holding tight, he fought the swallow.

The predator shook its head violently, trying to dislodge the shrimp. Shareef held on. He dug his pincers deeper into the flesh. Then he spotted what looked to be a soft part of the palette. He could see it clearly. It was almost lit up for him, so Shareef released one of his pincers, reached across the mouth and tried to grab on before he could be shaken free. The shrimp never regained his grip. He even released his other pincer. There was something much more interesting than the soft flesh inside the mouth. There was light. The predator's head was no longer shaking and its mouth was wide opened. Before you could say "kelp," Shareef shot through the opened jaws.

He burst into the relatively open water of the tank and dove into the hidden cup coral, hunkering down where he couldn't be seen, where his life force couldn't be detected. Shareef peered out from the coral cover. There was a large angelfish hovering above some rocks. It took a moment to regain its senses and then resumed rummaging. Rocks and sand were tossed in all directions. Occasionally, the angelfish would stop, chew for a moment, and then get right back to work. He acted as though the little interlude with the shrimp had never happened. And that's what really bothered Shareef. How could this fish not acknowledge that he had almost swallowed the shrimp?

The more Shareef thought about it, the more upset he became. The crabby crustacean crawled to the rim of the coral cup, ranting, "You sucked up my rock, and tried to swallow me. I was in your mouth... and no apology? What kind of fish does that?"

The angelfish stopped feeding. He rose up and looked in the shrimp's direction.

"Yeah, you! I'm talking to you, rock sucker! You almost killed me," Shareef called. He swam out into the tank, until he was eye stalks to snout with the angel. He punctuated his protest by poking at the much larger fish with his antennae. "I'm fine, in case you're wondering, but that might interrupt your feeding. Wouldn't want to do that."

The angel spoke up, saying, "Well, you know—"

"I'm not done yet! Who chews their food, spits it out and then leaves it to suffer? How do you know I'm not hurt? I suppose it takes too much effort to come find me and check? Chew me up and spit me out? Nice. I just left an anorexic coelacanth and the next thing I meet is a bulimic angelfish. Ain't that a kick in the carapace?"

"Really?" was all the angelfish could say.

"Yeah, really. I mean, what's next? Will some cannibalistic cousin hiding in that weird coral attack me? What a place..."

"No, not 'really' that this has happened to you. And by the way, sorry about that chewing thing. It's been a long time since I've uncovered something alive. In here, I only find scraps from other meals, sometimes a spot of algae. And don't tell anyone, but at night, once in a while, I'll sneak a bite of sponge. I shouldn't, I know, but I just can't control myself. So when I uncovered you, I had no idea you were alive, that is, until you clamped onto the inside of my mouth. As soon as I realized you were in there, I opened up."

"Thanks."

"No, it's my mistake, totally. I probably should've checked up on you, but you flew out of my mouth so fast, you seemed okay. I didn't really think you wanted any more time with me, so I just went back to scrapping. My name's Pagre."

"I'm Shareef. So what was that 'really' about?"

"I probably didn't hear you right, but did you say you just left a coelacanth?"

"Yeah, Maputa."

"She *is* in here, isn't she?"

"Yup. I took those long dark tunnels. They seem to connect a bunch of tanks. This is the first tank, other than the one with Maputa, I've visited. It was almost my last one too."

"Again, sorry about that. So what are you up to? Why are you taking the tubes?"

"I don't know, for a little adventure, something different. Maybe one of these tubes will get me out of here."

The angelfish swam a bit closer, still keeping his distance so as not to scare the shrimp. While he could easily become alarmed, fear was not something the shrimp often succumbed to. Pagre said, "Don't look to the tubes for salvation. They will only carry you in circles. They will tease you. They will take you to different tanks, but they will never set you free."

"You look a little large to be telling me about what's in those tubes. How do you know?"

"I don't know anything, and yet, I know some things." The fish smiled. "I know if I keep turning these rocks over, I will find food. And I will be doing in here, what I would be doing out there. It is what the spirit has put me in the sea to do."

"Well, I'm guessing the spirit hasn't put me here to spend my life in a tank."

Pagre spit a pebble past Shareef, "Don't be so sure. That

might be exactly what the spirit wants."

"Not the spirit-fish that I know," the shrimp countered.

"Then perhaps you don't know him," the angel replied. As he began to swim away, Pagre turned back and said, "Tell the canth that I'll see her soon."

Shareef shook his antennae and said out loud, "Not likely, unless there's a tube the size of a turtle. And I haven't found that one yet."

Niv and Nhoj were in the midst of an intense phinball game. They played almost everyday, but today was special. The girl who had joined them in their tank weeks before, who had come to visit them daily, was serving the ball from beyond the tank.

Phinball was the dolphins' creation. They loved games. In the wild, dolphins would occasionally take a fresh kill, or a capture, or even some man-tide garbage and use it to play games. The dolphin brothers at SeaTopia, either through some visual stimulus provided by the man-tide or some latent game playing drive wired into their DNA, created phinball.

The closest equivalent the man-tide might know would be basketball, with fibers of soccer, volleyball and football woven into the fabric of the game. One player would be served the ball, a wet rubber basketball that was usually floating in the tank. Usually, Mom would do the honors, but on rare occasions a human who would actually visit the dolphins when they weren't performing could be coerced into playing.

Today, for example, Nhoj had noticed that Samantha was sitting in the empty bleachers. At times, he could be quite devious, especially when he wanted something. At the moment, Nhoj wanted to play phinball. While Mom wasn't really in the mood for the swimming, shooting, scoring, slamfest, Niv was always ready to take on his brother. But who to throw the ball? That's when they spotted Samantha.

It was a quiet Saturday at SeaTopia. The girl was sitting in a shaded part of the bleachers, the only shade on the tank. The dolphins were almost always in the sun. It made them a bit uncomfortable, but guests could see them better in the underwater viewing windows.

Samantha was busy scribbling in her notebook when she felt it, the first drops of the daily afternoon rain had come a bit early. The heavy drops hit her pages. Freshly laid ink blotted and streaked down the paper. Clouds could gather quickly on the warm shore. Samantha looked into the sky, but there were no clouds. The wind napped. The sun was firmly in control.

More drops. Samantha took one in the eye. It stung. The girl shook her head and rubbed the eye, thinking, "Acid rain, wonderful." The water cascaded down her face, cooling her cheek as it slipped into the corner of her mouth. She felt it on her tongue and tasted salt. Samantha looked away from the sky and scanned the stadium. Then it landed in her lap, knocking her notebook into a small puddle at her feet. The laughter that followed was unmistakable.

The dolphins had been splashing her. When they realized that she was not "getting" it, Nhoj tossed the wet basketball at her with impressive accuracy. The girl dried off her notebook, tucked it into her backpack and consulted her watch. Her lunch break wasn't nearly over. The rain mystery solved, she prepared for a little Phinball, although she knew neither the name nor the rules of the game.

Samantha picked up the ball and bounced it once, splashing herself when it landed in the puddle below, followed by more cackling from the dolphins. Unsure who tossed it at her, she threw the ball to Niv. The game was underway.

What the dolphins understood, was that the nearest one of them must catch this pass. The other could not interfere, unless they were equidistant from the toss. Niv caught the ball easily in his opened jaws. Then he slipped it under his chin and dribbled it by pushing down and catching it in the upsurge beneath his lower jaw. He did this continuously as he rounded the tank.

But Nhoj had other thoughts for the ball. He bore down on his younger brother, determined to rid him of the rubber sphere. In order to avoid a flagrant fin penalty, Nohj had to accomplish his task without slamming his brother excessively, a concept he constantly grappled with. The older brother's dorsal fin cut through the water, a silver line traced his track. Nhoj would grab the ball on Niv's next push. The ball slid off Niv's chin. Nhoj lined it up and threw himself—into his mother. She nudged him off to the side, whispering, "He's younger than you; be fair."

"He's the only one here. I don't have many options," the disgruntled dolphin protested.

"Shh," his mother whistled.

In the meantime, Niv was engrossed in the game. He was coming to the end of his lap. A decision needed to be made. He would rise up and then choose between Samantha, or the hoop the hung over the edge of the tank. The first option was some type of shot; a forehead roll, a jaw jam, three-sixty, one-eighty, reverse fluke flip or one of the countless other shots he and his brother created could be attempted. The successful toss would earn him two points. Niv's other option was to pass the ball to the man-tide beyond the tank. If it was caught, one point.

Nhoj, who had slipped away from Mom after a steady stream of less than convincing "yes, Moms," could legally challenge the shot, but not the pass. He raced to the rim to prepare for his brother.

Niv liked scoring on Nhoj. Nothing felt quite so satisfying as faking the defender, letting the ball fly, seeing it pierce the hoop and then serenely slap the surface. One of the reasons they both liked this game so much was because the net that hung from the hoop served as a perfect model for all nets. It had a nice big hole in it.

A pass to the man-tide might be thrown freely, but a lot depended on an outsider's ability to catch the slippery ball. Niv decided he would let the game come to him and finprovise in the air. He caught his last dribble, took the ball as deep as he could and exploded towards the surface. Blessed with whistling pops, he came completely out of the water, saw the hoop undefinded and released a soft coral curl shot. The ball climbed a bit higher, disappeared in the glare of the sun, and then emerged a breath from the hoop, right on target.

Nhoj had every sense at his disposal locked on the ball. He threw himself completely at it, tucked his head toward the water and swatted it with his tail flukes. The ball changed direction, and quickly left the tank over the far wall. But before Nhoj could celebrate, as he usually did, dancing on his tail, fins in the air... he saw a perplexing smile on his brother's face. The ball was in Samantha's hands. Nhoj had tipped it toward her and she had caught the ball. "Point to Niv," mother announced.

Niv was pleased.

"Style points! Style points!" Nhoj protested. "Did you see that inverted swat? Big air, sweet swat, tasty twist... Gimmie some love! Style points, please!"

Mom, a softer touch than a wet sponge, considered the request. Nodding, she acquiesced, "Okay, *one* point for style."

After one shot, he dolphin brothers were tied. Mom would do her best to see that it ended that way. The small tank only got smaller when one brother won and the other lost.

Samantha stayed and played Phinball for the remainder of her break. When she returned to work, she was as drenched as the dolphins; the wet ball soaking her every time she caught it.

On her way back to work, Dave passed, stopped and asked, "Been swimming with the dolphins again? We have wet suits for that."

"Kinda," Samantha smiled. "But I never entered the tank."

No stranger to Phinball himself, Dave, whose name-tag read Dave-phin, after all, knew what had happened. Changing the subject, he said, "I heard your mother got the grand tour last evening."

"Yeah, I thought it was time she saw where I was working and what I was doing."

Dave was disappointed that it was Samantha who thought it was time, that her mother hadn't shown the interest on her own. But trying to keep a good face on the moment, he said, "I heard she went for a little swim with the dolphins. Did she fall in like you?"

"No," Samantha smiled. "Allison was with us, so I thought it would be okay."

"You had Ally-gator with you? I'm amazed she let you near *her* dolphins."

"It was kinda weird," Samantha confessed, "the mother dolphin kept rubbing up against my mom. She pretty much ignored me and Ally, but she was like in love with my mom."

"That's a strange one," Dave agreed, on several levels. "Maybe it's a mom thing."

It *was* a mom thing. As soon as the human mom entered the water, the dolphin mom scanned her and the other two humans with her sense of sonar. Dolphins did it to all creatures that crossed their paths. Janee was attracted to Samantha's mother because when she scanned the one human, she actually saw two. Samantha's mother was pregnant, and the only ones in the tank who knew were the dolphins.

Cariam had made his way back into the large predator tank. It was not a place he wanted to visit, but the tank was the closest to the beach, which meant it was the closest to the sea. If he was going to make a break for it, the proximity of the tank could make all the difference.

The octopus had turned a muted aqua-blue, with traces of thin white scattered along his smooth skin. He hugged the wall of the tank and followed a shaded shaft in a remote corner toward the surface. With two hundred suckers on each of his eight arms, he climbed the wall effortlessly. Cariam could have easily swum to the surface, or climbed much quicker, but he didn't want to be seen. He was in a vulnerable position, exposed. His boneless body might prove too tempting for the sharks and others who circled the dead coral.

The octopus pulled himself above the waterline. Immediately, he felt the sun touch his bare wet flesh. If he was going to escape, he realized, it would have to be at night, or at least early morning when the tank blocked the sun and the air was still cool. Cariam pulled back his mantle and raised his eyes over the wall. He could see the ocean clearly. Like when the moon hung huge in the night sky, he felt as though he could reach out and touch it. But like that very same moon, the ocean was a world away. It would take more than the stretch of an arm to feel freedom, especially if he was bringing a pudgy stargazer with him.

Cariam studied the water, its motion, its reach. He tried to find the spot where it came closest to the tank, where the least amount of beach would have to be covered to reach the sea. He would plan his escape for the next full moon. If the sea swelled and swallowed some of the sand, it might make the job easier.

Relieved to re-enter the water, Cariam lowered himself back into the tank. There was planning to be done. He slid down the slippery wall, wondering whether Norton would join him, or perhaps stay with Pagre. The latter was difficult to imagine, but a possibility nonetheless. Once he reached the sandy floor, Cariam crawled into a hard purple sponge, assuming its color and form.

"You'll never make it," the octopus heard. "I know what you're thinking—thought it myself, seen it before—but I'm telling you, you'll never make it."

The words seemed to bubble up from the sand. Cariam could not locate their source. He waited.

"Ask one of the turtles what it was like to emerge from the nest and make that first dash, one they could make a lot faster than you by the way, into the sea."

"Who is speaking? And what are you talking about?" the octopus asked.

"I'm a friend. And you know what I'm talking about. I watched you…"

"If you are a friend, show yourself."

It was often true on the reef, but in these tanks it was a constant; the coral has eyes, the sand has ears and the water echoes.

A gill gently fanned some sand as it took in a bit of water. A faint dusty puff rose and drifted off. The voice followed. "You would think that once you got out of the tank, all your troubles would be over, but really, my friend, that's just the beginning."

Cariam could tell where the words were coming from. He turned one arm tan, slipped it onto the sand and stretched it towards the source. He could feel the vibrations of voice, breath, even heartbeat pulsing through the sediment. He knew exactly where his "friend" was hiding. But what to do? He waited.

"Don't worry. I'm not hiding from you, I'm hiding from them."

The octopus scanned his surroundings. He saw nothing alarming, nothing suspicious. The predators swam in mindless circles. Fins followed the same worn path in the same water around the same coral. No one seemed interested or aware of his presence.

"You'll never make it alone. And you better hope Seacusea doesn't hear about it, or you'll get out of this tank, all right."

"Well, the less you talk about it, even though I still don't know what it is you're talking about, the less anyone will hear of it… friend."

"Ya mean it?" Out of the sand slid a flat, tan sole. It approached the purple sponge, repeating, "Ya mean it? We are friends?"

"I've seen you before, in the other tank. Yes, Finbar. You

swim in both tanks?"

"Why not? So do you. And there are many of us who can get away with it. Must be pretty easy for you, an octopus and all."

"What do you mean, 'get away with it?'"

"When you live here, you have to pick a tank: Reefs or predators. Either one suits me, although it's a bit more relaxing over there."

"So why are you here?"

"Change a' sand, I guess. Never know what you'll hear, what you'll see. Take today for instance…"

In an instant Cariam threw out two arms, raised up the one in the sand and suckered down on the flounder. He whipped the fish deep into the dark coral and pounced on him, enveloping him beneath his mantle. "What's your problem, Finbar?"

"What d'ya mean! Nothing! Lemme go," he mumbled from beneath the fleshy hood that engulfed him.

"Clam down." The octopus loosened his grasp. His point was made. "Mind your own scales," Cariam warned. "Okay, friend?" With that, he released the sole.

"Okay, I didn't mean anything. I've been here long enough to see some things; thought maybe I could save you a little trouble. That's all."

The octopus listened.

"I mean, we are friends, right?" Finbar asked anxiously.

"Sure we are," Cariam tested.

"I'm betting you plan to go at night. That might save you from the sun and from being spotted during the day, but you'll have problems at night too."

"Well, if I was gonna try something like that, and I'm not mind you…"

"So you've said."

"… what problems are you talking about?"

"There's plenty of 'em. First, you'll have to deal with the raccoons, the cats, the rats, a dog perhaps, possum maybe.

They're all out there at night. And you don't even have a shell like the turtles."

"What are raccoons and…"

"You don't want to know, believe me." The flounder lowered his voice, yet it added volume to his words. "I'm betting you will wait for high tide, which will shorten your run, eh, more like a crawl for you, but like most things, it will add other problems."

"How could a shorter beach be a problem? I mean if I actually—"

"Yeah, right. We're talking hypothetically, I know. Listen, if you go at high tide, it'll probably be a full moon. That's almost as bad as going in daylight. And you know how the full moon makes the ocean predators a little, shall we say, unpredictable? Well, it does the same for the ones on land. You'll have full moon predators in here *and* out there. I'm not sure a new moon would be much better, maybe too dark. You got problems."

The octopus looked around once more. "You got any answers, or are you just good at finding problems?"

"I'm good at lots of stuff," Finbar grinned.

Dorfman sat at the edge of the tank with his feet immersed in the cool water. It took the edge off the hot day. As he gazed into the pool, he turned his toes in small circles.

"I wouldn't do that," Kemar said as he approached.

"Feels pretty good."

"It might not feel so good if the canth decides it's feeding time."

"I don't think she'll be interested in these feet. Maybe if we rubbed them with some of that squid over there."

Kemar nodded, "No, I guess she's not really eating much of anything. Maybe it wouldn't be so bad if she tasted those toes. Want me to get the squid?"

Dorfman casually withdrew his feet from the water. "Any

thoughts?"

"I have lots of thoughts. What I could use are answers. I don't like her color, or her behavior."

"The water is perfect. Seventeen degrees centigrade, which allows a fish with such a slow metabolism to draw plenty of oxygen from the water. It's just what it would be off the Comoros."

"Could it be the pressure?" the young Cambodian asked the professor.

"I really doubt that. This fish has a swim bladder that is filled with oil."

Kemar nodded, "So the oil isn't affected by changes in pressure like an air bladder would be in most other fish."

The professor grinned. He was gaining more respect for the skinny whiz-kid. "I'm thinking maybe it's the light..." They both looked up immediately at the blazing sun overhead.

"But she's in the cave all day. How could the sun be a factor?"

"I'm not sure. We're guessing, remember? Her eyes are more like a cat than a fish. She lives in the dark where she sees just fine."

"You think," Kemar continued, "she's in the cave to get away from the sun? That she'd really rather be out in the open water?"

Dorfman nodded. "I'll bet when that sun hits the water, especially from overhead, it's like looking into a permanent flash. I'll bet she's blinded. Heck, I'll bet even a full moon could be uncomfortable for her."

"Yes," the boy agreed, "and it must be almost impossible to feed when you're blind."

"Yes and no," the professor said. "She can eat just fine without eyes in her head, provided she can rely on her rostral organ."

"Right, it would pick up any electrical charge that crossed its path. Dr. Campbell told me it would even give the canth a sort of night vision, where the electro-receptor in the snout would enable it to 'see' its surroundings, regardless of depth."

"Okay, now let's apply it to this tank. Our canth is blinded by the sun, yet it should still be able to sense its food, but it's not."

"I know why!" Kemar called out like an excited child in school, which in a sense, is exactly what he was.

Dorfman, who reminded Kemar of one of his uncles, smiled and cocked his head, inviting the answer.

"There is no electric charge to detect. We're feeding her dead food! She can't see it because of the sun and she can't sense it because there's no pulse."

The professor laid his suntanned hand on the boy's shoulder. "You might have something there. Now, what are we going to do about it?"

Kemar looked up at the wooden coelacanth that adorned the entrance to the exhibit. "It seems Mr. Smitty had a good idea when he suggested live food. Can we get some squid, live?"

"Anything else she might identify with?"

"Dr. Campbell and I found eels, skates, sharks and cardinalfish in specimens that we've dissected."

"Good job, Kemar. We can get all those. There's a fella named Paul Gaffney who captains the *Hawkaye*. I'll tell him what we need and I'll bet we'll have a living smorgasbord by tomorrow or the next day."

"Perhaps Mr. Smitty will provide some shade for the tank and we will provide live food…. By the way, what's a borgasmord?"

Dorfman laughed, "I'll take you to one tonight, kid."

Shareef re-entered the tunnels. Right away, he realized that the return trip would be much quicker, much easier than his original trek beyond his tank. The shrimp glided effortlessly, occasionally bumping a side or a small mound of muck. "Nothing like an exoskeleton," he said to himself.

Shareef zipped along, enjoying the trip until he passed the opening to a tunnel… and then another one. Moving at this speed in the dark tubes presented a very different perspective than the struggle to crawl against the flow. Everything happened quickly. Shareef wasn't sure when to turn. He had no idea where he was. He was being carried, but to where? The shrimp discovered another alarming reality when he tried to stop, and couldn't. Caught up in the current, the momentum made it impossible for him to get a leg-hold. Every time he tried, the pointed tips of his walking legs slipped from the loose mud that lined the tunnel. The current captured the shrimp.

Eventually, Shareef turned it over to Seaqoyit. He gave up to the surge, waiting to see where it would end. He hoped he would not wind up pinned to some hard mesh like the ticks and fleas he had seen along the way. With a little luck, he thought, this might be a ride back to Maputa. He'd even settle for an express right back to the angelfish. The tumbling shrimp tried not to think of the negative possibilities, but one found him nonetheless.

The flow increased. The tunnel widened. Like streams running into a river, the tighter tunnels were depositing their flow into a larger tunnel. The further along he went, the faster the current swept through the tube. And the wider the tunnel became, the more difficult it was to catch hold, to slow down. Other debris had joined Shareef. Scales, clam shards, dirt, small stones, parasites and other things rumbled around the current, bouncing off the shrimp. And from what little he could see, or sense, he was the only living thing among the collection.

Finally, just as before, there was a faint glimmer. The water ran towards it. Once again, there was light at the end of the tunnel. The shrimp allowed himself to hope. His moment was coming. Would he be delivered to life or death? For an instant his mind wandered, amused that the reality of being tossed into another tank would actually represent the life side of the equation, replacing his quest for freedom in the open ocean. Compared to death, the tanks seemed pretty good to him right about now.

And then he hit it. Hard. He was pinned against it by the press of the water. The stones, the shards, all his companions in the current began to bounce off his body. Pressed against a tight, hard mesh, the shrimp was being pummeled. The thick dirty water was difficult to breathe. All the waste from all the tanks came crashing down on him. Shareef had wanted an adventure, and he had found one.

Chapter Four

Keepers or Catch & Release?

It had been a hot and cloudless day for the dolphins. Their sparse open tank provided nothing in the way of shelter or distraction. Round, smooth and exposed; it was an endless open circle. One color, one shape, one size, one depth, one view, one temperature, one way, everyday. The Spirit was surely testing them.

When the sun finally settled into its union with the sea, relief came... and so did activity. And what better activity than a quick round of Phinball before the dark took over? Without anyone from the man-tide to help, it was up to Janee to serve the ball. This was a two sided sand dollar. On the one side, she did enjoy athletic activities, especially with her sons. But on the other side, no matter what she did, she would be perceived as favoring one of her children. Often the game ended with each of the brothers claiming the other got preferential treatment. But after a day in the sun performing mindless tricks, the freedom, the spontaneity of sport was just what they all needed.

In his own subtle way, Nhoj would grab the ball in his mouth and push it, almost gently, into his mother's side, relentlessly restless, until she got the message and agreed to play the game. Even if she got mad and chased her son around the tank, nipping and knocking, that was okay with Nhoj. Any attention, negative or otherwise, suited him just fine.

When mom tossed the ball into the tank she always did it backwards. She didn't want to see where her boys were—one less way to accuse her of finvoritism. Niv, her youngest, had a habit of towing an old rubber boat bumper in his mouth, the way a small child would carry its blankie. In fact, the whistle and click he used to refer to it, translated from dolphin into man-tide, meant ballie. It was the young dolphin's security and he didn't readily relinquish it. Even when it wasn't in his mouth, he always knew precisely where ballie was. But when mom picked up the orange Phinball and assumed the position opposite the hoop, Niv spit out ballie like a rotten mackerel. He and his brother raced around the tank, loosening up their fins like taking lay-ups before tip-off.

When they were ready, they waited at the center of the tank. Mom leaned forward and then snapped her head back, lobbing the ball between them. The ball struck the water with a slap. And before the sound could echo off the wet wall, both brothers were pressing against each other, fighting for the first shot. The ball and the players disappeared underwater in a swirl of churning fins.

The ball returned to the surface, a mouth emerged and pulled it down. Then Nohj burst from the bottom, breaking through the surface, hurling himself into the air. He lined up a blow-hole roll for a two point shot because he didn't trust that mom would try her hardest to catch his pass. Nohj rolled the ball out of his mouth, over his upper jaw and forehead. When it hit his blow-hole, he sucked in as hard as he could. The suction held the ball in place. He'd do a half spin, like his cousins the spinners, and while hanging upside down over the rim would release suction and blow the ball into the basket. It would be a gaudy, nudibranch of a move, something any player could brag about for days, although with Nhoj it would probably stretch into weeks.

The phinball fantasy, however, came to a crushing demise when the ball was pulled free. It popped off as Niv threw himself across his brother, grabbed the ball in his teeth and wrestled it from the blow-hole. Then he turned in the air and tossed it to mom. The ball bounced off her back and rolled out of the tank. Phinball, at least for this evening, was over.

The youngsters raced to their mother to protest her lack of

concentration. How could she possibly be looking out of the tank when a game was in session?

"Hello? Niv to mom, a little game going on here."

"Well, the ball's gone now," Nhoj added. "Gonna be a real exciting night without—"

"Shh!" Janee raised a fin. "Listen… do you hear it?"

The youngsters listened. They looked at each other. They listened some more. Above the grind of the surf against the sand, beneath the peep of the osprey combing the shore and right next to the thump of the pelicans pounding the mullet that rose to the surface, they did hear something. A dolphin.

Mother and sons, hanging over the edge of their tank, looked out to sea. The sun was slipping away behind them. The shadows were long and the light had dimmed, bowing to the dawning dusk. Occasionally, when they breached above the walls of the tank and the seats of the diminutive stadium, the dolphins could look out over the sea. And occasionally, they spotted free dolphins exploring the shoreline. The dolphins came and went. They fed, played and socialized. Then they disappeared. In the beginning of their captivity, Janee and her little ones would call out to the passing pods. In the beginning, a dolphin or two might call back, wave and move on. But over time, Janee stopped calling to them. And over time, they stopped waving to her.

Tonight, however, a dolphin was calling, and it seemed that Janee knew who it was. In a moment, she was airborne, higher than her sons had ever seen her climb. At the apex of her lift she seemed to hang in the air. She wailed a loud call to the dolphin, and then crashed back into the tank, weeping. Without a word, she was back into the air. This time she saw him. Onaro, her mate, had arrived.

He had found them. He was out there. He called to his family.

Janee turned to her sons, "Jump! Jump! Like never before! See your father! Onaro has come!"

He swam closer and they all could see him clearer. He was large, but not the largest; strong, but not the strongest; fast, but not the fastest; smart, but not the smartest. Still, the combined effects of all these valuable traits made Onaro extremely formidable. Ignoring the surf, he launched himself above the breakers. The boys instantly felt safer, calmer, stronger. They did not know it, but when he saw them all together, alive, Onaro also felt safer and stronger.

Ally-gator noticed the dolphins' agitation. She blew a whistle and signaled them to her side. When it went ignored and unnoticed, she called for help.

Onaro and his family jumped continuously. They were in the air together, underwater apart... in the air together, underwater apart... in the air together. They called to each other, until all four were rising and falling in some strange synchronized connection. Their unison bridged the tank, the boardwalk, the beach and the shallow surf that separated them.

The man-tide gathered around the tank, observing the display and wondering what could be done. The dolphins were crazed like they had never seen before. A vet, scientists, trainers and others discussed the display. Were they suffering? Was it a disease? What was the bizarre behavior? They began to chat about sedation of the animals, for their own protection, of course. At that point, Dave took over. He directed the trainers to watch carefully, while he had the vet prepare sedative darts, which were only to be used as an absolute life-saving measure. Short of that, everyone watched and waited.

The dolphins were concerned with only one thing, the moment. They had seized it. They were swimming with father, mate—calling, crashing, splashing, over and over and over. When they were finally done, exhausted and sore, the sun completely set, Janee laid her head on the deck of the tank and quietly sang his name. She would not stop, and neither would her sons, for this was the first time in their lives that they could hear and see each other as a family.

The sun was gone, replaced by a moonless dark sky. Clouds gathered and rolled silently over the sparkling stars, extinguishing their illumination. The three in captivity could no longer see Onaro. He no longer called to them.

They had never felt so alone.

Would he return? Would he remember? Janee and her sons did not know, but they hoped. They wondered whether Onaro would stay. He could live his life right out there in the surf and see his family, call to them. Would he make that choice? Perhaps, he would visit at certain times or tides. At the very least, they knew now that Onaro was waiting for them, out there, somewhere.

Elaine and John began almost every day of their golden years walking the beach. They arrived early, parked their car, a '64 Plymouth with push-button transmission, that was designated as the "beach buggy," right on the flat sand, always avoiding the turtle nesting sites. The newer, nicer Buick stayed safely tucked away in the garage, where salt and sand could not infect the purity of Detroit's finest.

The two opened their folding chairs, John lit a cigar and Elaine combed the tidal pools for fresh shells, which she'd send to her grandchildren as treasures from the sea.

But really, Elaine was hopeful that even at this early morning hour, a jogger, a biker or a walker, would stop and say hello. She would tell them all about her family and would listen to their story as well. Elaine was not one of those people who used others just to talk about herself. She was genuinely interested in all of them; a retired first grade teacher who was convinced that there was good in everyone. And if you didn't know where it was, she'd find it for you. She took in all the glory of the sea, and then shared it with everyone who crossed her path.

John had a slightly different outlook. A World War II veteran and a retired New York police officer, he was less than fascinated by everyone else. What held his complete attention at this hour was a fascinating White Owl; the cigar, not the bird. It was all the interaction he required. Well, that's not completely true. John was with Elaine, as he had been since the seventh grade, and he was happy.

After she had gathered her shells, after he had finished his cigar, the two, who were one, slipped fingers between fingers and laid palm against palm, joining hands to stroll the flat cool shore.

It was not uncommon to stumble upon a confused gopher tortoise heading towards the surf, or occasionally, an equally confused sea turtle hatchling heading into the traffic lane. In each case, the animal would be lifted and returned to the safety of sand dune or surf. The two seniors had also rescued injured pelicans, terns, wrens and too many gulls to count.

But today, for the first time, they encountered a creature they had never seen on the sand before.

The seniors froze when they spotted him. A large dark dolphin, covered with sand, lay on his belly while the surf receded behind him. He was dry. A high-pitched moan floated quietly on the breeze.

Flustered, Elaine looked to her police officer husband, who had served in the Marine Unit for many years, although he had never arrested any dolphins. He had to shoot a shark once, but that was about the extent of his interaction with sea life.

John scanned the beach. He could see the blue Plymouth behind them. He could see SeaTopia in front of them. And the one time *he* wanted to see someone else, there was no one. Then he remembered a friend who lived around the corner was a handy man at the aquarium.

"Elaine, listen, get up on the boardwalk and find Smitty at the aquarium. Tell him what's going on and bring help."

His wife nodded and made her way to the boards. She

climbed the stairs, looked back and saw John running in and out of the surf, his wide straw hat full of water as he poured it over the dying dolphin.

Cariam waited until he was sure that the sole was gone. He could not decide whether the fish was friend or foe. The octopus thought about the advice he had been given. The cautions, whatever their motivation, seemed real. "Could it actually be safer in here than out there?" he wondered. The octopus looked up at the sun above the tank. Clouds had rolled in, veiling the oppressive glare. A thought began to trickle inside his mantle when the inspiration was interrupted.

A head emerged from the flat wall of the tank. A fish was entering from the tube. Norton was searching for his friend. The gazer surreptitiously slipped down the smooth surface and nestled himself beneath the sand. Only his eyes were visible, and they scanned the tank for signs of Cariam. When the octopus saw the gazer looking his way, he quickly pulsed red throughout his body. Soon Norton had joined him in the coral.

"You said you wouldn't leave without me," the fish began.

"And does it look like I've left? I'm still here."

"But you're planning something, and it doesn't look like I'm in the shell on this one." It was an opportunity, an opening for Cariam to bring his friend up to speed.

"I'm always planning something, you know that. It's my nature."

Norton smiled, "Yeah, the price you pay for that huge mantle…"

Cariam removed a piece of floating algae from that very same mantle. It was a strange plant; green, alive, but not like anything the inhabitants of Makoona or SeaTopia had ever seen before. While there were fish here from all over the world, none had seen this plant before. It grew at an incredible rate and none of the creatures could eat it, except for a dainty slug from one of the smaller tanks. The algae was confusing, both natural and unnatural at the same time.

"You know," Cariam confessed, "I said I'd take you with me when… if I escaped, but I'm not even sure who *you* are, really."

"What?"

"I mean, suddenly you're putting a lot of importance on what some angelfish says. All of a sudden you're into this whole spirit fish thing. It kinda gets in the way."

Norton nodded, "I see. You say the spirit gets in the way. I'm thinking, it is the way."

"Okay, so what's that mean? Does it mean you don't think for yourself anymore? You do whatever you're told? You just sit around and accept whatever happens to you and rationalize it by saying it's the spirit's will?"

"I don't think it means that at all. I didn't let you just leave. I came after you. I could have easily said that it was the will of the spirit that you left. I live my life, but in a way, it's not my life anymore. I think coming here showed me that. It's the spirit's life *and* it's my life. We sort of live it together."

"But that's what I'm talking about—"

"Let me finish. What I'm trying to say is that by being brought here, I see that it's not *just* my life, that the spirit and I share everything that I do, all that I am. Pagre gets that, and I'm starting to."

"Well, does the spirit tell you to stay or go, because what I'm hearing in my heart—"

"Which one, you have three," the gazer couldn't help himself from joking.

"Always with cracks. Listen, I'm serious. What I'm hearing inside is, *get out!* And I think I can do it… I think *we* can do it."

"Listening to what's inside can be a good thing, provided you listen carefully…"

"And you think I'm not?'

Norton raised a ventral fin, "I didn't say that. Let me tell you what *I'm* hearing inside. I would never, could never, tell you what to do, but I think there's something that must be done before either of us leaves this place, before either of us is allowed to. But once it is done, we will leave and we will have help."

The octopus flashed dark green. It was the mollusk's equivalent of a nod.

Norton stretched open a single gill cover. The scale that Pagre had offered Cariam fell slowly to the sand. "Deliver this to the canth. She needs it. The spirit wants her to have it. You have been blessed with the ability. Do this and we will leave."

An arm reached out, a tiny end-sucker seized the scale and it was pulled into the coral. Cariam flipped it up and down. The two watched a small shaft of light tickle the translucent orb. It seemed to hold the light, store it inside. After a moment, the octopus came closer. "You want me to deliver this to the canth and *then* we can leave?"

Norton grinned.

"You do realize that I don't know where this so called fish is? I don't know what it will do to me when I arrive, if I arrive. I'm supposed to do this, and *then* I get to *try* to escape? I gotta tell ya, pal, I think it'll be a lot easier just cutting to the escape part and skipping this whole mission or calling or whatever you want to label it."

"You know how sometimes you can search for food all night," the gazer suggested, "and then, the moment you give up looking, you find something to eat?"

"We're not talking about food."

"What I'm saying is that sometimes, when you stop putting yourself first, there's a freedom in that, and you actually get more for yourself by worrying less about yourself."

"But no one's asking *you* to do this. This one's about *me*."

"That's my point," both ventral fins were lowered and opened. "It's not only about you. This one's about the canth, the spirit, and doing the right thing. Go for it. Answer the call."

The exasperated octopus flashed a deep dark purple. He raised one of his arms, pointed the tip at his friend and said with conviction, "I am gonna answer the call. I am gonna go for it."

"You're going to the canth? "Norton asked hopefully.

"I'm going, but not to the canth. I'm going home, back to Makoona. You coming, pal?"

Norton shook his head.

The octopus turned tan to match the sand and slid to the base of the wall. When he got there, he turned pale blue, slapped a few hundred suckers on the smooth surface and started climbing. The shadow of the bull shark passed across Cariam's body as he rose closer to the surface. He looked beneath the shark to see if either it or the remora that hung just below its gill slits was aware of his presence.

Norton also noticed the passing shark. He rustled the sand where he sat, trying to get the predator's attention, so that his friend could escape unnoticed. The shark lowered its pass. The remora twitched beneath it: a signal, perhaps, that something required investigation. Norton tried to judge whether he could make it to the hole in the wall that led to the reef tank if the burly bull became too curious. Norton was quick, but not fast. It would be close. He slipped into the coral and waited.

Just as the gazer returned his gaze to the octopus, he saw delicate ripples roll outward in succession. The sun sparkled as the clear ridges of water struck the side of the tank. Cariam was breaking through the water, leaving the tank in broad daylight.

"There's nothing else I can do," Norton lamented. He was about to pray for Seaqoyit to carry his friend back to Makoona when the water exploded.

At almost the same moment, the bull burst into the foamy patch on the surface. It threw its head side to side, slashing with opened jaws and exposed teeth. The remora beneath held fast and Norton thought he glimpsed, through the churning, a shifty grin on its face.

While all eyes, and tentacles, turned toward the fray, Norton used the distraction to shoot into the hole in the wall that led to the tube that connected the predator and reef tanks. From there, he would be safer, yet closer to the action should his friend need him. And it certainly seemed like Cariam needed Norton.

When the bull shark withdrew, still shaking his head as if something were caught in his teeth, the water settled. The barracudas were the first to investigate. The jacks would follow. It would be a little while, if at all, before Norton had the chance to examine what was left. That probably wouldn't be necessary.

The gazer knew water wasn't very good at holding most clues. There was, however, one clue that Norton had detected. It was the type of clue water was actually very good at preserving, other liquids. Norton could taste it. There was blood in the water. Then he saw it, a minute translucent cloud. Little more than a puff, floating in the water, dispersing slowly under much larger clouds that swept across the sky. There was no mistaking it. Norton saw it and tasted it. Dark blue blood from an octopus had spilled into the tank.

Norton turned to the shark. The animal was agitated. Something was making it very uncomfortable. It gagged and choked. He watched as the bull rubbed its face against the dead coral, brushed his teeth into the sandy floor and pounded his snout against a rock. Eventually, the remora, who seemed less than enthused, released itself and inched toward the mouth. "Hold still," Norton heard the fish say. "Let me have a look."

Sharks do not like to "hold still." They need to move to breathe and the bull was in no mood for more discomfort. Silently, it swam to a spot in the tank that always had a fresh current, a spring of sea water. The shark positioned itself so that the current ran across its gills. Then it opened its mouth.

Ever so slowly, the remora entered the tooth-lined cavity, hoping that a nervous twitch, an unexpected spasm or just a sudden realization that the remora would be more useful in its stomach than hanging from its chest didn't strike the shark. More parasite than cleaner in character, Seacusea gently, very gently, scoured the jaws of its host.

A strange "Ah-ha!" echoed from the shark. It was strange, Norton thought, because although it came from the shark's mouth, it was the voice of the remora. A second later, the fish burst from within, clutching something in its mouth.

The shark seemed relaxed. It grinned, opened and closed its jaws once or twice and grinned again. It nodded to the remora. "What was it?" the bull asked in deep quiet voice. The remora laid them on a rock and then swam back into position under the shark.

Norton couldn't see very well, so he poked his head a little further out of the tube. It was dangerous, but he just had to see what was left of his friend before the others consumed the remains. The gazer's eyes grew wide when he saw what was on the rock. A half dozen feathers danced in the current that spewed from the wall. The feathers were large, white and gray. They tumbled in the torrent while a group of grunts picked at the tiny shreds of flesh that clung to the quills.

The gazer was confused. It tasted and saw blood, octopus blood. And yet, there were feathers. The fish looked back to where Cariam had disappeared. The water was still, until a raindrop popped on its surface. A moment later another fell. Taking a chance, Norton swam into the spot. A drop fell onto his face. Then he froze. Another drop hit the water and Norton swallowed it. "This is not rain," he thought. The gazer swallowed again. He ran the water across his gills and under his scales. It was raining blood.

Blood was falling into the tank. Norton raced to the wall. He used it to brace himself while he tried to get his eyes above the surface. He was very scared. The sight of the water exploding was still fresh in his mind. He did not want to add gazer blood to the trickle that entered the tank. There was danger from below as well. Even this small amount of blood in the water could set off a feeding frenzy. It didn't take much for the sharks to get worked up. The hammerhead began swimming excited loops. The sensory organs located across its face were looking for prey. The barracuda were always on edge and the tank was stuffed with a host of other lethal residents, but Norton had to know what happened to his friend.

He saw it as soon as his face broke the surface. The blood was coming from Cariam, dripping into the tank, and also from an osprey whose talons were deep into the octopus' flesh. The bird circled in the sky, not too far above the tank. A bloodied wing had been clipped by the shark. The raptor labored to stay aloft and escape with its prize. Climbing higher into the sky, it headed out over the beach, trying to reach its nest. But Cariam wasn't finished just yet. He wrapped his arms around the bird. Suction didn't work too well on feathers, but if he could encircle the osprey and lay one arm against another, he could use suction against his own skin to ratchet arm over arm to squeeze the bird; forcing the air from its lungs, breaking bones if necessary, like a boa constricts its prey.

Norton watched the octopus, knowing exactly what his friend was thinking. The arms connected. The octopus squeezed. And the bird dropped Cariam.

It was one of those moments when you cheer and scream at the same time. His friend was released. "Be careful what you wish for," the gazer thought to himself. Now the octopus, arms flailing, was plummeting to earth, perhaps to his death. Cariam disappeared from sight before he hit the ground. Norton saw several birds gather above the spot where he believed his friend had landed, but that was all he could see. The gazer slid back into the tank, said a prayer for Cariam and swam toward the tube that led to the reef. "Maybe Cariam went home faster than he thought he would," Norton reflected.

Onaro opened his eyes and saw nothing but blue. Above him, below him, all around him there was nothing but blue. It was bright, beautiful, and for the moment, relaxing. It should have been perplexing, however, it wasn't. The dolphin knew where he was. He had no idea what he was going to do, but at least he knew where he was. Sore and groggy, Onaro felt physically like one hundred waves had slammed him into rocky cliffs. On the inside, he felt like he had eaten way too many mullet. He was nauseous. It hurt to open and close his blow hole. It hurt to breathe. It hurt to swim. It hurt to think. There wasn't much that didn't hurt Onaro.

One thing, however, made him feel good. He was as close to his family as he'd ever been. He would find a way to meet Niv, the son he had never met. He would embrace Nhoj, the son who had grown without a father to guide him. And he would swim away with Janee as he had once done when they were younger. This time, he would never leave their side.

The dolphin swam slowly, circling the tank. Eventually, he was drawn to a shaded spot, where the freshly rising sun cast a cool curtain across part of the tank. The cold felt good. It numbed and soothed.

"They might not know who you are, but I sure do," Onaro heard a voice whisper. There was nothing else in the tank. He scanned the water with vision, echolocation and every other sense at his disposal. He was alone.

"Over here. It's your neighbor."

The voice sounded close. Onaro poked his head above the water and over the side. The thump of pain pulsing through his body suggested that this might be more work than it was worth, but the dolphin needed to know who was speaking to him.

Just as he laid his head on the side of the tank, another head appeared across from him. It was the manatee. "Welcome," she smiled. "I don't usually say this to new arrivals, but in this case it might prove true. Nice to meet you."

Onaro's curiosity got the better of him. "Why wouldn't it be *nice* to meet me?"

"No, no, don't take it the wrong way. I didn't mean it like that. It's just that arriving in a place like this is not usually a pleasant experience. And so, I'm usually sad to meet someone here. It means they're no longer out there." The manatee nodded toward the sea.

"That makes sense. So why, in my case, are you happy to meet me?"

"Well, it's kinda like my friend on the other side over there, Gilgongo. If he didn't show up here, he would've died. So, I was happy to meet him because it meant he would live."

"And you thought I would die if I wasn't here?"

"I did see you when they dragged you in. And to tell you the truth, if you didn't wake up this morning, I wouldn't have been surprised. But there's a better reason why I'm happy to see you." The manatee smiled again. A piece of lettuce was stuck to one of her teeth, an unsightly patch of green against her otherwise pearly teeth until she removed it with a lazy swipe of her tongue.

"You gonna tell me about this better reason?"

"We both know the reason. Don't forget, I'm a mammal too. I know what went on the other night. I can hear."

"So you know who I am?" the dolphin probed.

"I know who you are," the manatee looked over at the dolphin stadium, "and I know who they are."

"Then you must also know why I'm here," Onaro tested.

A tear came to the manatee's eye. It welled up and dropped onto the cement beneath her. "You beached yourself to be with them, your family." She sniffled. "It's so rofishtic. It's beautiful. How can I help?"

Onaro nodded, a gesture to acknowledge that the manatee did indeed know his purpose, but there was more to the dolphin's visit. While he absolutely wanted to be reunited with his family, he had no intentions of remaining in captivity. "One way or another, sooner or later," he clicked to himself, "we're all gonna get out of here."

"Shh," Naillij said, and she slipped back into the water.

Initially, the dolphin was perplexed. But the moment he felt them, he too slipped back into the water, where he was in charge. Onaro had been touched. Samantha approached quietly, reached down and stroked him gently.

"It's okay," she said softly. "Just wanted to say hello." She dropped a frozen mullet into the water and Onaro, never one to eat scraps tossed from the man-tide's floating islands, watched it float to the bottom. He thrust his tail flukes twice and was instantly at the other end of the pool. A safe distance away, he paced, keeping an eye on the visitor.

For the first time in her life, Samantha had encountered a truly wild dolphin. She could see right away that he was not like the three who she played with daily. Part of her wished that this wild one could see her with the others, see that they were friends and that this human would not hurt any of them.

Deciding that this was as good a time as any for a lunch break, even though it was 8:45 a.m., Samantha sat down, dangled her feet in the water and scribbled into her notebook. She wanted the tired dolphin to see that people would not hurt him and understand that he was not alone.

Samantha was also not alone. Kemar walked along the side of the pool toward her, although his eyes were on Onaro. "Manta-Ray," he smiled.

"It's *Samantha*-Ray, K-Mart," she shot back.

"K-Mart?"

"Well, if you can call me 'Manta-Ray', then I'm calling you K-Mart. Butcher my name, and I'll butcher yours."

"Yes, *Samantha*, I will be more careful…"

Ever since they first met at the coelacanth tank, Kemar and Samantha found themselves running into each other. Samantha found the chance meetings one of the best parts of her day. Kemar would agree with half that. He too enjoyed the brief encounters, but from his perspective, they weren't exactly chance.

Kemar knelt down next to his friend. "I'll show you mine if you show me yours?" he said.

"What?!"

He looked at Samantha, puzzled by her reaction, "The bag... I carry one too. I'll show you what's in mine, if you show me what's in yours?"

"Even that's a little personal, don't you think?"

"If I thought that, why would I have proposed it?"

Samantha couldn't quite tell if Kemar was legitimately confused—which wasn't difficult to imagine—or if he was teasing her. Either way, she enjoyed the exchange. "I have no desire to see what's in your bag," she declared.

"You might not say that if you knew what was in here." Kemar produced a small blue felt sack from beneath his vest. It was the definition of weathered, yet it still looked solid, clean. Every tatter was trimmed back. A new chord had been strung through the top. It was a simple sack, yet Kemar held it with such respect, his friend could see that whatever this bag contained could never be replaced. The more she looked at it, the more she had to know what was inside. And that's precisely what Kemar had intended. "Show me yours, I'll show you mine," he whispered.

Onaro sneezed. A wet spray from his blow hole caught the seaside breeze. Droplets skipped across the tank and splashed into Samantha's face. Both Onaro and Kemar smiled... perhaps for the same reason. The embarrassment of the moment had broken the spell of the blue bag. Samantha was not going to be seduced by the faded velvet. She would not share her secret with someone who took pleasure in seeing dolphin drool splattered across her face. Samantha wrapped both arms around her equally weathered and venerated backpack. The gesture was not lost on Kemar.

He reached back and plucked a towel that was draped over a cooler, handing it to his dripping friend. When she did not accept it, he leaned over to wipe her face. Only then did Samantha release her grip on her bag and snatch the towel.

The sun lit up Kemar's face. His teeth sparkled as he spoke. "I tell you what. Why don't I toss you a frisbee."

"What are you talking about?" Samantha giggled.

"You know, a frisbee. I will give you something, for free. You don't have to do anything..."

"Not a 'frisbee,' you knucklehead. You mean a 'freebee.'"

"No, I think I mean a frisbee. On this matter I'm quite sure of myself... My English is sometimes licking, but I know frisbee."

Again, Samantha could not tell whether Kemar was serious or joking. One of the reasons, she realized, was that inside he seemed to enjoy everything. Even when he was serious, there was always this muted joy. It was there even when he was absorbed in his science, so it was almost impossible to know when he was kidding. And although he was becoming a young man, there was this boyishness about him, an aura almost, that she knew would still be there when he was old.

Samantha-Ray conceded, "Okay, your English is definitely not *licking*. Go ahead, toss me a frisbee."

Kemar slipped a hand back into his vest. He took out the velvet bag and laid it carefully on the cement between them. As he untied the shoelace that held it closed, he said, "Your bag is your bag, this is mine. No treasures in here for others, but no treasures anywhere else for me." Kemar reached into the sack. He withdrew his hand, palm down, his thumb tucked underneath, holding something. He held his hand over Samantha's. She opened her fingers. A pair of delicate wire rimmed glasses fell into her hand. They were as worn as the bag that spawned them, and yet they were immaculate. The girl looked at her friend, waiting for his words.

"My father's," he said.

Samantha nodded. She heard much more in his voice. She could tell that it was a memorial, a piece of the past, that Father was gone.

"I like to look through them sometimes. I don't need glasses, but they still help me see."

Samantha handed them back to her friend. He nodded, inviting her to try them on. "Should I?" she asked.

Kemar nodded again.

Samantha handed the glasses back to the boy in a way that suggested she was unworthy rather than not interested. She was still young and this was confusing. The sun was getting higher. The day was getting hotter. Streaks of gold dripped from the sky and washed across her hair that bounced in the breeze.

Kemar returned the glasses and handed Samantha something else from the bag. It was a thin sheet, several actually, folded like paper, but they were metal, like tin foil. However, these were gold, not silver. The reflection of the sun exploded across the sheets. They warmed quickly and launched the tiny rays in all directions as they moved in Samantha's small hands. "They're beautiful. What are they?"

"They're called taels. Where I come from, back in Cambodia and on Makoona, these are money. They're made out of gold."

"Why do you keep them with you? SeaTopia must be paying you... a lot more than I get, I'm sure."

"Most of them are in safer hands than mine, but I like to have a few with me. I may not need them, but I feel projected with them."

"Projected?"

"Yes, safer, more secure."

"Right, *projected*." Samantha didn't even want to try. She looked out at the dolphin. "Do you think he'll stay?"

Someone from behind them answered. "The more you sit with your feet in the water and the more you two hang around, the more likely he'll have to stay."

They turned to see Dr. Dorfman slipping on a pair of sandals.

"Didn't want to lose these. Left them here when we brought him in."

Samantha lifted her feet from the water.

"Sorry, Ray..." She would allow Dr. Dorfman that liberty with her name, but no one called her Sam—not and lived to tell about it. "Don't wanna get in the way, but this is, at least at the moment, a *wild* dolphin. And, for the moment, it's probably best to keep him that way. If he gets too used to us, he gets a life sentence in SeaTopia. Keep your distance and maybe we can reintroduce our friend after the vet clears him."

"I'm sorry," Samantha apologized.

"No apologies necessary, Ray. Live and learn, right? Come on, let's go."

The three gathered their things and left the dolphin. Onaro didn't mind.

Droplets and wind are a funny thing. As the wind increased, the droplets morphed into mist and were carried beyond Onaro's tank. Some of the mist settled on the dry cement between the tanks of SeaTopia. Some of the mist was carried over the railing on the boardwalk, landing on the salty sand. A few drops, however, were changed into a mist that clung to the breeze, finding their way to a face other than Samantha's. They moistened the cheek of Janee, who floated on top of the water listening carefully. She had hoped to hear something, but she never expected this. Her head snapped to attention. She felt the wind on the right side of her face, turned into it and froze.

A phinball splashed behind Janee, washing the mist from her face. Niv and Nhoj let the ball float away and turned their attention to their mother.

"I can taste him," she said softly.

"She's getting wavy," Niv said to his brother.

"Quiet, he's still here."

"You mean, Dad?"

"I just got wind-washed and I tasted him."

Nhoj burst into the air, hung for a moment and splashed down. "I'll start looking."

"Me too," added Niv.

But their mother stopped them. "I don't think he's out *there*."

"Well," Nhoj said looking around the tank, "he's not in here."

Janee looked concerned. "I think he might be. The breeze that delivered the taste came from the west. If Onaro was in the ocean it should have come from the east."

"So he's not here?" Niv turned a tight circle of his head to suggest that he meant the tank. "But he is *here*?" He followed with a grander circle that referred to the larger aquarium. Janee nodded.

"Finsome! That's totally tubed!" Nhoj whistled.

"I'm not so sure," Janee muttered.

"Be careful what you wish for," the octopus thought to himself, invoking the same saying Norton had. The osprey responded to Cariam's constrictions by opening his talons and releasing his catch.

Cariam was blown away by the speed with which he plummeted; the air pressing against bare skin… nothing between him and the ground below. It was terrifying, beyond the imagination of a sea creature. The constant support, the buoyancy of water was nowhere to be found. Cariam braced his boneless body for the impact.

WHAPPPP!

Stunned, he laid flat in the sun and closed his eyes. The

octopus wondered what organs he had ruptured and waited for the pain to set in. The irony did not escape him that he was almost free, a hopeful crawl from the open sea, and yet he could not move. The sun on his skin no longer burned. The heat did not dry his flesh. Cariam began to feel cool and wet. "At least I died out here and not in there," he thought. "This is what must happen before you meet the spirit." And then Cariam remembered another saying both he and Norton were familiar with: Everyone believes in the spirit when they are on their death seabed. "Oh great," he lamented, "I'm about to meet the spirit I just said 'no' to."

Cariam heard a voice. "Do me a favor and don't eat me. I'm *so* close."

The octopus opened his eyes and saw a little shrimp darting across his face. Cariam raised his mantle and saw something else. He was in a small tidal pool.

"Look, I just got outta there a couple days ago. A tunnel spit me onto the beach at night and I popped around until I landed in a puddle. A little more popping, a few more puddles and the next thing you know, I'm in this tidal pool. Been here for a day and a half."

Cariam was too weak, too shocked to say anything. He turned tan, backed into a corner and listened.

"Nothing's eaten me yet, I guess you can see that, so please gimme a pass. I mean the moon's gonna be full tonight. I'm sure high tide will reach us. And then, we both get outta here. You're not hungry, right?"

"You were in there?"

"Yeah, my name's Shareef. I'm not from around here. I came with a canth and she's—"

"You what?"

"A canth… a coelacanth. You've probably never seen one, but I came with one named—"

"Maputa…"

"Whoa, that's a little freaky," Shareef replied. "How'd you know that?"

Cariam had no idea how he knew the name. "I'm a little freaked out, my—*not again!*"

The water exploded. Sharp talons gripped one of the arms that Cariam raised to shield his mantle. They dug deep into his flesh and pulled the octopus from the pool.

Shareef watched from what he assumed was a safe distance. He yelled, "Good luck—" An arm whipped toward him and a tiny sucker pinched down on his back; gently, but firmly taking hold. "Aw, come on, give me a breaker, why me?"

Cariam took the shrimp with him. "I'll tell you later."

"If there is a later."

The osprey was persistent. A meal as tasty as an octopus could not be relinquished without a second try. Again, it flew into the air high above the beach. The octopus dangled from a single leg pierced by the talons. The bird held tight. It would not allow its prey to get a grip and squeeze as it had last time. Suddenly a gull swooped in and took a peck at Cariam. Another did the same.

Shareef screamed, "Why me? Why do I have to be here? At least release *me*!"

"I need to talk to you," Cariam explained.

"Don't think that's gonna happen!"

A tern spotted the meal and flew in for a taste, forcing the osprey to change direction. It headed over SeaTopia. By now, most of the birds on the beach had spotted the flying meal. The osprey was so weighed down by Cariam that they gathered beneath him and took turns pecking at the octopus. The osprey would not let go.

Cariam had his own thoughts on the matter. He screamed "Hold on!" to Shareef and then he did the opposite. The octopus released his arm from his body. It was a defense mechanism his kind would use in the sea. When an eel or some other predator snatched an octopus it would often give up an arm and then swim off. The arm would regenerate, the predator would eat and the octopus would live. It is precisely the principle that Cariam applied to his current situation. Since the osprey would not release him, he released it.

He and Shareef were free. They were plummeting, escaping to SeaTopia. The pair hoped that they would hit something soft, like water. Looking down, quickly comparing the surface water of the tanks to the amount of hard ground between them, Cariam estimated they had about a seventy-five percent chance in favor of the harder impact. And before he could consider it further, they hit.

For the second time in a row, the octopus drew water. He and the shrimp splashed down hard and sunk to the bottom. When he touched the sand, Cariam released his companion. The octopus laid flat. He had pain on top of pain. It was all he could do to change color, blending with the brown-blue bottom. Gathering his thoughts, Cariam could not believe he was back in SeaTopia, back in a tank, one he had not seen before. He wondered who inhabited the cold water. Would some monstrous predator he'd never seen before appear and swallow him? Although, at this point, he felt like something had already done that, chewing him up real good before it swallowed.

Cariam pumped up his mantle a bit and raised his eyes. They were staring right back at him, a shell away from his face. He could taste the water coming from its gills as it washed across his body, which in many ways functioned like a giant sensor. A pair of green glowing eyes stared lifelessly down. Just as he had thought a moment before, it was a monster. An enormous mouth with jagged teeth; not unlike a moray's teeth, but much larger, faced him, agape. Was this creature smiling? And if so, was it happy to have a visitor, or perhaps tickled that it would have a fresh, unscheduled feed. The rest of the fish was huge. It hovered above him with its head pointed down. Cariam was afraid to move. He tried not to breathe. But none of that mattered. This fish knew exactly where the octopus was, exactly what it was. It was locked onto the electrical pulse of life that flowed through Cariam. There was no way to hide.

The seven-armed octopus wondered if the stump of the eighth arm was leeching his blue blood into the water when he had an idea. Ink. If he could blast a load of ink into the face of this fish, and jet away into cover before he was swallowed, he might escape. The ink would hide his whereabouts and it would interfere with the monster's ability to smell. But Cariam would have to hide beneath rock, or in an inaccessible crevice to stay safe, because sooner or later, especially locked in a tank, the fish would sense the electric within him.

Cariam prepared to execute the plan. He shifted the sack so the ink would have maximum effect. He aimed his siphon against the sand. It would blow sediment up into the cloud, enhancing it. And when he squeezed the siphon, the water would blast into the hard bottom adding to the lift as he propelled himself away from the mouth, which would surely be thrust downward where the octopus sat. Cariam counted to himself, "One… two…"

"Hey, Maputa," Shareef said.

The fish turned toward the shrimp.

"This is Maputa?" Cariam was stunned. "This is what the spirit wants me to help?"

"Yeah, this is Maputa." Shareef smiled and looked at the canth. "Do me a favor, will ya?"

"What do you need?" Maputa asked.

"Eat this guy, will ya? You won't believe what he just did to me. Besides, he's an octopus, no bones, you'll love 'em."

"I know he's an octopus. What's he doing here? And where were you?"

"Just eat him. I can tell you all that stuff later. I'd eat him myself, but it'd take a while…"

The canth finned a bit closer to Cariam. She almost touched

him when she asked, "Did you say something—and don't worry, I'm not going to eat you—"

"Oh great," Shareef lamented.

"—about Seaqoyit sending you here?"

"Ah, yeah, I guess I did," Cariam replied.

"Don't listen to him. He's lying!" the shrimp interrupted.

"I am not!"

"Yes, you are, you told me the spirit asked you to come, but you said no, that you decided to escape for yourself instead."

"Then why am I here now?"

"Because an osprey dropped you in here *by accident!*" Shareef screamed.

"There are no accidents," Maputa mumbled, "and you cannot say 'no' to Seaqoyit. If you are here, he sent you."

"It wasn't even Seaqoyit!" The shrimp refused to relent. "Some angelfish told him that the spirit wanted him here. He got it second fin."

Cariam turned reddish brown. He could be seen plainly against the brown-blue bottom, as if to illustrate that he had nothing to hide, that he was being completely honest. "It is an angel. His name is Pagre. My friend Norton also asked me to come see you. They said it was the spirit's will."

"Apparently is was," the canth added.

"But I don't really know why I'm here. I don't know what they expected me to—wait a wave, Pagre asked me to give you this." Cariam stretched out an arm. A small sucker at the tip opened up and a tiny scale flashed in the water.

"He obviously pulled that off himself," Shareef said. "Nice try, mollusk."

Maputa turned to her friend, shook her head slowly and said softly, "He doesn't have any scales... Hold it up to my eyes."

Cariam raised the scale up to the glowing eyes. The canth studied it. She flashed that weird smile and opened her mouth. "Lay it in my mouth."

"How about I just put it down and you pick it up yourself?"

"I won't hurt you. You were asked to deliver the scale, now deliver it into my mouth."

"I don't want to lose any more arms today," Cariam said as he stretched his arm as far as it could go.

"Go ahead. Let's see what Seaqoyit has in mind." Suddenly Maputa snapped up the scale. It happened so fast, the octopus's arm was still extended while she swallowed.

"Okay," Cariam said, "that was pretty scary. Could you warn me the next time you're gonna do something like that?"

"What fun would that—" The canth and the shrimp looked at each other and then stared at the octopus. Cariam followed the line of their gaze. They were fixed on the stub of his missing arm. Slowly, but noticeably, it was growing. What would have taken over a month was returning to full size in moments.

"Whoa…" was the best Shareef could muster.

"Does it hurt?" Maputa asked.

The octopus shook his mantle no.

Maputa looked away, as if she was listening to something. The others heard nothing. The canth nodded, looked at her companions and said, "Seaqoyit is coming."

It was a beautiful dusk, not a cloud in the sky. A warm breeze waded across the sea. However, beneath the surface of the planet there was restless turbulence. Miles away, miles below, beyond the continental shelf, an eruption caused two plates to collide, forcing one plate to rise above the other. The unexpected displacement of water created a surge that raced toward the shelf. When it reached the suddenly shallow water above the cliffs, the energy from the plates was transformed into a rogue wave of modestly massive size. The wave gathered speed and rolled on. It had no mind of its own, but that's not to say it had no mind.

And there was definitely a destination. Had the surfers some advance notice, the more daring among them would have waited in giddy anticipation. There were others who would've also hailed the arrival of the water, but to them the ocean meant much more than a tasty tube.

The sun was just about swallowed by the sea. The visitors had all gone. The only people left were a few of the staff completing their chores. Many of the free animals had also left, but no one really noticed. Raccoons, other small mammals, tortoise, lizards, nesting plovers, even insects began to move away from the beach, SeaTopia and the area around it. Fish who inhabited the shoreline swam north, others moved south. Those who listen to the planet, like these animals, often hear things coming. That is why they were going.

The more shallow the water became, the bigger the wave grew. Luckily, boats and bathers were nowhere to be found. The wave rolled on.

One of the first to realize what was coming, Gilgongo stretched his head above the surface and climbed half out of his tank to get a better view. Immediately, he saw the animals leaving. Everything became a bit too still, a bit too quiet. It was all the confirmation he needed. The turtle climbed back into the water and swam to Naillij.

"If there's any food laying around in your water, eat. You might not get another meal for a little while."

"They'll bring more in the morning, they always do," the manatee replied.

"Maybe not tomorrow morning."

"Of course they will."

"Shh," the turtle interrupted, "do you feel it?"

Naillij's eyes grew as wide as sand dollars. "*No...* do you think?"

The turtle nodded. "Tell the dolphin. Let's swim the word."

Naillij paddled across her tank, quite quickly for a manatee. Onaro was waiting for her. He looked concerned.

"You *know*. I thought you'd be happy."

"I am happy, but I'd feel a lot better about this if I was over there." He gestured toward the dolphin stadium. "It might not even reach."

"Might not," Naillij nodded, "but what if it does?"

A deep dolphin grin creased his slick face.

When Norton entered the tunnel that led to the reef tank, someone was in there waiting for him. The remora, Seacuesea, blocked his path. "If you like my water so much, why are you leaving?" he hissed.

The gazer tried to squeeze into the hole. He felt very vulnerable floating so exposed in open water. The hammerhead searching the sand below added to Norton's discomfort. "I have done nothing to you, Seacuesea, nothing to anyone. Why are you impeding me? Let me enter."

"Strange things seem to happen when you are around. Why don't you explain what you and the octopus are up to? Then, when I'm satisfied, you will return to your tunnel."

The gazer couldn't help but notice that the repulsive remora had bad breath, probably the result of a lifetime of breathing another's water, eating another's scraps. However it happened, the water that emanated from Seacusea's gills tasted like rancid muck at low tide. The stench drifted with him always, but was more pronounced in the confines of the tunnel.

Norton began to charge the pads behind his eyes. He had a shocking surprise for the remora if it would not be reasonable. "I'm not really worried whether you're satisfied."

"You should be, gazer. Because when I'm satisfied, *they're* satisfied."

It was obvious who *they* were, but Norton decided that he answered to something greater. He answered to Seaqoyit and he wanted to tell Pagre what had happened to Cariam.

The remora could not fill the tunnel totally. He was not as

large or as powerful as he liked to believe. And without being connected to the bull, he was just another unpleasant fish in the way. Had he asked nicely, the gazer might have discussed the matter. With circumstances the way they were, however, Norton juiced up the pads Seaqoyit had given him for situations just like this.

The way Norton hunted, bursting from a burrow in the sand, he could blast into action as fast as anything with scales. He threw himself at Seacuesea, veering into the space the remora could not fill. When the two fish were plastered against each other, Norton released an electrical charge that surged into the flesh of the nasty remora. It burned through the fish's nervous system, causing it to constrict into a tight ball that just happened to fill the tunnel completely.

Norton was bounced back out of the entrance. There was plenty of juice left. The gazer would try again, and again, until the remora, exhausted, could be brushed aside.

Before he could return to the battle, Norton was bashed into the side of the tank. Seacuesea smiled as the gazer was pinned against the wall. The bull had arrived.

All Norton could see was teeth. They were all around him, rows and rows, white and twisted. He knew what had happened. He should have known better, did in fact, but everything was so different in the tanks. To the predators that electrical blast was as bright as a goby's stripe. All hungry eyes were on Norton, at least on the tiny bit of tail fin that protruded from the side of the bull's mouth.

Reattached beneath the gills of the shark, Seacuesea spoke first. "I get this feeling that you're going to tell us all about what's happening with you and the octopus."

"He doesn't need to. I will," a voice answered. Pagre approached the danger.

"The angel of the god who allowed the man-tide to take us and keep us here speaks," the remora mocked. "He has not been beyond these walls for tides, yet he knows what Seaqoyit wants. Let's have our feed a bit early. Begin with the gazer and then on to the angel, doesn't that sound good?"

"If that's your plan," Pagre answered, "start with angel, but let me speak first."

The bull released Norton, who sunk to the bottom. He turned to Pagre, sizing up the angel. In a half hiss, half whisper, Seacuesea hisspered, "His scales are much more nourishing than his words."

The bull shook its head, violently severing the suction of the remora, who joined Norton on the bottom of the tank. "Seacuesea does not speak for me, although he likes to make others think he does. Sometimes that's helpful, other times, like now, it's not." The shark looked down and said, "He will be quiet, but what are you here to say?"

"There are two reasons for my visit. I don't want any harm to come to Norton."

The bull considered the first request. He had no reason to hurt the gazer. He also had no reason to test Pagre's connection to the spirit. And lastly, he kind of enjoyed watching the gazer shock Seacuesea. The shark nodded in agreement. It was Pagre's signal to continue.

"The other reason for my visit is to tell you two things."

"Do these *things* come from Seaqoyit?" a barracuda asked.

The angel shrugged his fins. "What do you think? You know, Seaqoyit lets me hear your prayers. I know what everyone asks for. I know who doesn't pray. I know who does and tries to hide it. You want to leave. You hate the man-tide. You hate Seaqoyit. And you are not fishtians.

"I will tell you the truth. You could have, should have, found it yourselves. The man-tide did not take you. You were given to them. You were chosen by Seaqoyit. We have our balance, they have theirs. For the most part, we do not invade them, but the man-tide can be brutal to us. The islands they float on the sea bring death to fishtians. Your spirit knows this. It happens, largely, because the man-tide does not know you. Your pain is not real. Your beauty is ignored. Your life is misunderstood, devalued. And since the man-tide will not live with you, you must live with them.

"Seaqoyit chose you to represent your brothers and sisters. Your beauty, your grace will save lives. You are not alone. Others have been chosen, others will be chosen. This is a beginning, not an end. You have been called, by your spirit, to bring the sea to those on land, to remind them that neither of us are alone. In this place, *we* become the fishers of men. We are here to capture their hearts. You remind them that we are here together, sharing one world."

As the angel spoke, others bowed their heads, raised their fins or assumed different postures of prayer. "A-fish," one moray said in agreement.

"You said there were two things you wanted to tell us. What is your other message?" the bull inquired.

"Oh, yes, I almost forgot. Keep awake for you do not know when the master of the sea will come. I say to you all, keep awake. Seaqoyit loves you. You are his chosen."

"That's it?" the hammerhead wondered. "The spirit loves us?"

"Oh, right, sorry. It's a lot to remember, you know. There is one last thing: You're free."

Every creature in the tank, in virtual unison, said, *"What?"*

But before the angel could elaborate, the wave arrived. He beamed as he said, "Thy will be done."

And it was.

Chapter Five

Surf's Up

It was night and no one was on the beach. Everyone had left SeaTopia. The land animals were either gone or hunkered down. The ghost crabs climbed into their holes. The osprey with the chewed wing made its way inland. The free fish had fled. Those in the tanks readied themselves. They were about to be reborn.

Before it broke and struck, the wave rose into the air, climbed high above the dunes, passed over the boardwalk, until it found SeaTopia. The water stretched from one end of the aquarium to the other and barely a foot beyond. And then, as if held by a string, it paused for a moment. Fish in the forward tanks could see the wall of water hanging above them. It eclipsed the moon, the stars, everything. Most ducked for cover, except for Pagre, who seemed quite pleased with the imminent devastation.

The two security guards had just finished making themselves ice cream sundaes when it hit. The impact threw them to the floor.

Miraculously, no one was hurt when the string was cut and the water crashed onto the tanks. Seaqoyit's version of a "smart bomb" had found its mark. Every tank on the premises was ripped open. Many creatures were picked up in the rush and carried away, tumbling and twisting. The water was blue-black; filled with sand, sediment and debris. Gear, frozen fish, souvenirs, tickets, programs, floated on the rivers of receding water as if they too were escaping from SeaTopia, like the rest of its inhabitants. But when the surge returned, only the stuff of SeaTopia came back. The sea life was gone.

Still, some creatures became trapped in cracks and stuck on dry spots. Not everyone had a merry swim to freedom. And there was danger. Heavy beams crashed into shallow water. Live electrical lines fell into pools and puddles. Other lethal debris was tossed about in the turbulent flow.

Naillij and Gilgongo slammed against each other. The manatee wondered if the turtle's newly healed shell would withstand the battering. A pair of sea lions riding the undertow raced out to the open ocean. The turtle's shell withstood the impact, but he was left upside down on dry ground several yards from the receding torrent. Upside down, he watched smaller, more nimble fish find freedom. Suddenly another wave rolled in. Much smaller than the initial strike, this comber had no trouble lifting Gilgongo, bouncing him off a bench and a flagpole before setting him down, again on dry land, but now right-side up.

Gilgongo understood the situation. He had done this before. Once. As a matter of fact, any turtle would see the similarities. Gilgongo was entering the ocean just as he had done when he emerged after hatching. Some of the dangers were different, some the same. One thing that was different this time around, Gilgongo was fifty times larger. No bird was going to fly off with him in the surf. No raccoon would come near him. No cobia was going to swallow him. The turtle was livin' large.

Female turtles left and entered the sea every time they laid a new clutch of eggs, but males were expected to make the sacred journey one time. Gilgongo raised his head halfway. He needed to see where he was going, but he didn't want to get hit with anything. He crawled as fast as he could, hoping to reach the water that ran back to the sea before more water pushed him back into SeaTopia. The water was swift enough and the fish were fast enough to escape quickly. For the turtle and, as he could see ahead of him, the manatee the journey was more arduous.

It was easier for the turtle than the manatee. Gilgongo was more streamlined and had a protective shell. Naillij was large, heavy, round and soft. There was no buoyancy for her in the shallow run. Her body was struck and pierced by floating debris.

"Are you okay?" Gilgongo called to her.

Naillij rolled on her side, so her tiny eyes could see the turtle. "I'm fine."

"But you're bleeding." Several red rivulets ran down her gray flanks and across her whiskered snout.

"It's only blood. I'm filled with the stuff. Luckily, I'm also well-cushioned. It may not be a shell, but fat gets the job done."

"Can you make it?" Gilgongo asked.

"I'm gonna try, but don't wait for me. There's nothing you can do."

"It is a long way, but I can push. I can make it shorter for you. Let's get into the deeper faster flow."

"No, I want to go the other way."

"There is no other way!" the turtle screamed. "There is only the sea. Let's go!"

"No," the manatee said quietly. "There is no sea, I want to go there." She pointed to a damaged tank, still two-thirds full of water. Everything inside had escaped. "I want to go back. I want to stay here."

"Oh, something must've smashed your skull," Gilgongo said in disbelief.

"You can return. I can't."

"Of course you can! That's what this is all about! Come on!"

"No, there's nothing out there for me. It's so difficult to find food. The turtle grass is all but gone. And it's too dangerous. No floating islands in here crashing into me, shattering my ribs and slicing at my skin. No debris wrapped around my fins, tightening and cutting to the bone. No nasty man-tide. The ones in here are different. They care about me."

Gilgongo looked at his reconstructed flipper. He nodded. "There is a pearl of truth in what you say. But I am meant to be out there and that is where I'm going."

"You should. I *was* meant to be out there, many, many tides ago. But today is not the tide of the manatee. Perhaps another day we will return, but not today." Naillij rolled herself over the side of the tank, fell into the water and smiled to her friend. "It's okay. Be happy for me. I am thrilled for you. Now go."

"I must…"

"I know." The manatee nodded her head toward the sea. "Go, be free."

Gilgongo watched the manatee's blood disappear from her wounds as it washed into the tank. He turned and went, sloshing his way toward the beach. Another turtle leaving tracks to the sea. When he was fully out of sight and Naillij was sure that she would not be a burden to her friend, she lifted herself up onto the damaged wall, onto the jagged, broken concrete and began her journey to the sea.

Two tanks over, Maputa called to Shareef and Cariam, "Come to me. Let's stick together!" The shrimp swam under the canth's gill cover and felt safe.

Cariam jetted himself over and climbed between the fish's unique ventral fins. He suckered down and flattened himself. His suckers were so powerful, the canth would have to lose its scales before it lost the octopus. In all the excitement and danger, Cariam could not help but marvel at the way Maputa's fins steered and steadied the huge fish. He had never seen swimming like this before.

"Will you be okay?" Maputa asked.

"No bones, no breaks; don't worry about me," the octopus replied.

Cariam returned the concern. "What about you, my ancient friend?"

Maputa smiled her snaggly, spiked smile, "I live under active volcanoes. This is nothing. It's what canths do. Just hang on."

"No problem. That's what octos do."

Back in the predator's tank, Pagre could see the fear in the remora's eyes. Its host was gone. Its false world had been obliterated. Seacuesea had no power out there. He was just another fish returning to a very large sea. The angel, however, took no joy in the creature's terror. Pagre swam to the remora, nestling next to him. It was not a time for preaching. It was a time to witness, so Pagre said nothing. He allowed the fish to see that he was not afraid. He hoped the spiritless gill tender would understand what was happening and see that with faith fishtians need not fear anything.

There were many other fishtians in SeaTopia who were afraid. And there was one who actually fought the undertow, who fought the opportunity to escape. It was the park's newest arrival, Onaro. He was not taken by the man-tide. He believed he was not chosen by Seaqoyit. He had come for a different reason.

The dolphin allowed the current to carry him out of his tank and past the dolphin stadium. Then he rode the secondary surge back into what was left of the aquarium, searching frantically for his family. Were they safe? Had they left without him? Did they even know he was here? How horrible it would be to lose them at this moment.

Onaro spotted a stargazer stuck in some sand where spartina grass was growing on a flattened dune. It was all underwater now. The fish was totally mesmerized by what had happened. He was laughing, shaking his head, talking to himself. "There goes a grouper! Home again, home again. There goes a nudibranch, a Regal Sea Goddess. Swim, nudi, swim!"

Norton loved nudis. They had all the beauty, all the protective toxin of coral, but none of the restrictions. They roamed at will. Their lives were ruled only by their whims. Norton watched the undulating purple and gold goddess swim off. It was the first sweet moment that he realized he was back in the sea. The gazer lamented. "If Cariam only lived another half-tide, he'd have been here with—"

"Hey," Onaro called. "Seen any dolphins swim by? A female and two young males?"

"I saw them," Norton answered. "Over there, where their tank used to be. The mother was chasing the youngsters, but they didn't look ready to—"

Onaro was gone. He fought the undertow while he waited for the surge to return and deliver him to Janee and the boys, his boys. He had heard Niv's name, and voice, for the first time when he called to his family a few nights before. Now he would get them all safely to the sea, or die trying.

He rode the surge, calling, searching.

"Forget it! Let's go!" Onaro heard. It was Janee. He saw her and was at her side in an instant. Their eyes met. For the briefest of moments they relished the reunion. But there was something much more important at fin. The surge was softening. They needed to leave while the swelling sea could still carry them. When the ocean calmed, if they had not seized the opportunity to escape, they would be stranded aground.

Onaro swam in between his sons. They were preoccupied with something, ignoring their mother's plea. Onaro turned to Janee. "The phinball. They won't leave without it!" she cried.

"What?!"

"They won't leave without it," Janee repeated. The look in her eyes, however, said much more. Onaro read them just as if they'd never been apart. Her eyes said, "This is your gene pool at work here. No one in my family gives a trout's anal fin about phinball."

The nagging, the accusations, the unfocused youths, the angry mate; it was his family all right. Onaro felt good. He dove under his sons and grabbed Nhoj's tail flukes with his teeth. He pulled at the youngster, trying to drag him away from the immutable ball.

Nhoj swung around. "Hey, ease up, Mom!" And then he saw

his father. Nhoj smiled and threw himself at Onaro, hugging and nuzzling. He reached out and batted Niv with his tail.

Niv whistled, "Are you crazy?! I almost had it! What are you—" Then he saw his father for the first time. He looked to his brother. Nhoj nodded and Niv flew into Onaro's fins. Janee joined them, reminding, requesting, "Can we leave now, before it's too late?"

Niv and Nhoj each grabbed onto one of their dad's fins. "Let's play some phinall!"

"Some what?"

"Phinball, Dad," Niv answered, the first time he had ever said dad. "It's this totally dorsal game that…"

"I know what Phinball is! You want dorsal, look out there. We can leave! Let's go!" Onaro yelled.

"But what about the ball, Dad? We can't leave it," Nhoj said.

At that point Janee and Onaro each grabbed one of the youngsters by a pectoral fin and dragged them away from the inaccessible phinball. "Don't worry," Dad said, "there's a million of them out there. We'll play tomorrow."

"Everyday!" Niv interrupted. "Hey, I want Dad to drag me. Why's he dragging Nhoj?"

"Now it starts. See what you've been missing?" Janee joked.

"I think after you're all safely in the sea," Onaro joked, "I'll just come back here and jump in one of the empty tanks."

"Not without me," Janee replied.

Dave was on his porch tossing lettuce to the wild iguanas that lived in the thicket when the wave hit. Stunned, he couldn't believe what he saw. It was a direct hit on the aquarium. He ran inside, grabbed his keys and started up his car. As he pulled out of the driveway, Kemar, who was staying in Dave's lower level guest room, jumped into the passenger seat. The two said nothing.

When they arrived at SeaTopia, Samantha was waiting at the entrance.

"What are you doing here?" Dave asked.

"My ride never showed," she said mindlessly.

Numb, the three entered SeaTopia. From the entrance to the front end of the snack bar and the souvenir shop everything seemed pretty much untouched, but when they came to the first tank, a ray petting and feeding exhibit, they saw what the wave had done. The rear end of the tank was gone and so were all the rays. Beyond the tank, everything was destroyed.

They stood there in disbelief.

"Where do we start?" Kemar asked.

"I could fire up the Whaler. I could call Captain Gaffney and have the *Hawkaye* look for some of the specimens, but what's the point? Even if we found any, where would we put them? The tanks are gone."

"The coelacanth!" Samantha gasped.

They ran to the spot where the exhibit should have been. "Wow…" Kemar shook his head. There was nothing there. "Looks like this is exactly where it hit."

"You know, when they built this place, years ago, right on the beach like this," Dave said, "I always thought it was cool, that we were kind of paying tribute to the ocean. But now, looking at all this, I'm wondering if we were mocking it, sort of shoving it in their face, you know, like taunting the sea?"

Kemar looked puzzled. "You think this happened for a reason? That the *sea* did this?"

"Right now, I don't know what to think. I think I might have to find a new job."

"Me too," Samantha agreed.

The three strolled around what was left of SeaTopia, waiting for the fire department, insurance adjusters, TV crews and others to arrive. They found themselves sitting at a small picnic bench. It was the only bench that escaped unscathed. A single light shone down on the table. Samantha laid her backpack on the surface. It was dryer than the ground.

"Would you show us that notebook now?" Kemar asked. He understood the severity of what had happened, but he had lived through devastation much worse than this in Cambodia. It had a way of tempering one's emotions. "Come on, what have you been scribbling the past few months?"

"Give her a break, Kemar. I'm sure Samantha—" Dave stood up. He looked out toward the ocean. A red lifeguard stand that had tumbled up and down the beach rested against a jetty. It was stuck between three very large rocks. Over and over, waves slammed into the stand and then tugged the frame as it ran back to sea. Dave climbed down from the table's perch onto the debris covered beach. Kemar and Samantha followed.

"Oh, I hope she's alive," Dave said as he approached the jetty. Then the others saw what he was talking about. The manatee was trapped inside the frame of the stand. She was rolling back and forth between the rocks, unable to escape the wood that surrounded her, unable to clear the incessant surf. The ocean tossed her bulk as if she weighed no more than an empty shell.

Dave picked up a stone and started pounding out some of the boards. Kemar and Samantha pulled them free once the nails were exposed. Soon the stand was dismantled and they could attend to the manatee.

Still alive, she was in bad shape, but not as bad as Dave had thought. The three pushed her away from the rocks. They tried to float her into a deep pool that formed behind the jetty. The manatee would not allow it. She forced herself down into the sand, spreading her flippers, making it impossible to move her.

"She's terrified," Samantha said.

"Yes, but I think she knows what she wants," Kemar added.

"Death?" Dave said. "You think she wants to die?"

"She wants to live."

"Well, that's what we're doing here, isn't it?" Samantha reminded her friend.

"Not to her," Kemar explained. "I think she wants to join all the others who escaped. She doesn't want to be floated back toward SeaTopia, she wants to clear the surf line."

"Can we help her do that?" Samantha agreed.

Dave nodded. He stood for a moment, rubbing his eyes. He kneeled down and looked into the manatee's determined face. Instinctively, he checked the identifying tag fastened to her rebuilt tail. "Okay, we'll get you out there, but the rest is up to you." Dave turned to his younger helpers, who were eager to release the manatee. He looked at them seriously and said, "Listen, this never happened. We're not doing this. Got it?"

There were no words, just nods.

"Let's do it, but be careful."

Using the jetty to brace themselves, they floated the manatee along one side, holding it off the rocks. As the water got deeper, the manatee seemed to understand what was happening and helped as much as she could. They carried her past the point of the jetty where she ducked behind the rocks, using them for cover while she angled herself out to calmer water beyond the rush.

Soaked, cold, the three returned to what was left of the aquarium. They sat down at the picnic table under the lone light pole. Samantha's backpack still rested on the table. Kemar reached out and tapped several times with a finger, smiling at the girl. "Come on, Samantha-Ray..." he teased. They felt a little better having helped the manatee to start a new life.

Kemar tapped the bag again.

Samantha untied the backpack and removed the notebook. She laid it down on the table and opened to the first two pages. "This is *my* SeaTopia," she said.

Dave and Kemar leaned over to take a closer look.

"It's an aquarium," she began. "Not one tank in the whole place. The closest thing is a man-made lake and a few canals...

All the animals can come and go as they like. Of course, we'd be limited to more local species, and some would appear seasonally or as they migrated, but every single creature could come and go as they pleased."

"Pretty cool," Dave said, "but expensive."

"Maybe not," Samantha replied. "We dig a series of canals that connect to the ocean and the intracoastal. Then we create habitats along the banks and in the canals themselves. Some of the spots we bait to attract specific residents. We use tunnels alongside and through the canals to view the habitats. We use glass-bottom boats and give tours."

"How would you see anything on cloudy days?" Kemar asked.

"We could light it up," Dave answered. "I did something like that for a friend on Big Pine Key. She lived on a canal, absolutely loved the wildlife, so I took two three hundred watt lights, waterproofed 'em, and mounted them in her canal. Tessa and I could sit on her porch and watch all kinds of sea life swim in and out of the canal."

"With a couple viewing stations under the water line, it wouldn't be much different than a tank," Kemar added.

"Except, we'd have no control over what there was to see."

"We would have some control," Samantha pointed out. "Based on how it was built and what plants and food we provided, we could attract targeted local species. You could even heat sections in the winter and see what gathered there."

"You could turn this place into a salt water lagoon with an inshore coral reef," the professional aquarist speculated. And then sizing up the destruction, added, "It's already half-way there."

Kemar and Dave grinned. They were impressed with the idea, but they were also impressed with Samantha. She sounded more like an aquarist with a graduate degree than a girl who fell into a dolphin tank one afternoon.

"We could build a man-made lake and do pretty much the

same thing there," she continued.

"But those animals couldn't come and go."

"No, but how many fish leave their lakes? If it was big enough and nice enough, they'd be a lot happier than in a tank."

"And really," Dave joined in, "it's probably the way these creatures should be seen. You know, in their natural environment."

"What if there were tanks?" Kemar suggested. "You know, just for injured animals who were being treated..."

"Sure," Samantha agreed, "or for ones that just couldn't be reintroduced."

"It'd be the most natural aquarium on the planet..."

"Except for the sea," Kemar quipped.

"What if all these canals are dug, all these plans are realized," Dave doubted, "and nothing came?"

"You mean animals or people?" Samantha asked.

"Both."

"If you build it, they will come. Both," the girl guaranteed.

Samantha had a host of other ideas: how to attract and display bird species, local reptiles, insects, and more. She suggested that there be a modest marina where visitors could climb into boats for tours and dives. There would be an theater where experts could lecture and people could see film of turtles laying eggs on the beach, migrating whales breaching off shore and countless other natural wonders that happened virtually on the site.

In the end, the eco-attraction would not be focused on specific marine or terrestrial habitats as much as it would reflect an eco-system, illustrating the webs of life that are still connected, even after they dip beneath the water or climb into the sky. Samantha had created, at least in her old *Flipper* notebook, something more than an aquarium, more than a zoo. She called it an Ecuarium. Kemar and Dave loved it.

Once Naillij cleared the jetty and the surf she was in pretty good shape. The slow moving manatee had quite a swim facing her, but she was powerful and patient. She stayed relatively close to the shoreline, out of the stronger currents, away from the larger predators, closer to food and shelter. Her only real fear was the smaller, faster-swimming islands of the man-tide. Staying close to the coast exposed her to more of them, but she had to do it.

Naillij listened carefully. She paid attention to every ripple and swell that crossed her whiskers or body. She would have to do that every moment of her life until she reached the spring, Blue Spring. Naillij swam north. The water was a bit cooler. Later, it would warm. When she came to the busier waters of the man-tide she would head west, inland, until she reached the river. Then she would swim south, against the flow, away from the mass of man-tide, quite a distance until she reached Blue Spring. For Naillij, the spring was heaven on earth. No swimming islands, plenty of turtle grass, lots of manatees. And best of all, the water was clean, clear, fresh. It was delivered to her kind from deep within the earth, warmed to a constant seventy-two degrees even on the coldest, cruelest winter day.

In winter, she would relax in the water with her friends and family. During cold months, thirty or even forty manatee would gather at the spring. When the weather warmed, they would disperse along the river. Even the man-tide, whom she could see watching from the banks, kept their distance and looked on with respect and awe. Shaded by oak and palm, everyday was a celebration. That was where the battered, tired manatee was going. In her mind, she was already there. Now it was just a matter of getting the rest of her to Blue Spring.

Naillij forgot about the salt, the oil, the fumes. She ducked under the swipe of the man-tide's racing islands. She set course and swam toward the spring. There were no walls now.

Chapter Six
Home Again, Home Again

Gilgongo couldn't help himself. As soon as he saw them, he had to stop. The turtle was on his way home. He was heading south toward the warm water, hoping to meet an old friend or relative along the way. But when he saw them, he forgot all about friends and relatives. He forgot about everything. Gilgongo had found sponges.

Yellow tube sponges, growing further north than he had ever seen, were clustered along a sunken ridge some thirty feet down. As large as Gilgongo; they were just waiting to be eaten. A soft green hue radiated off the enticing yellow. Masked gobies and cardinal fish fled from cover to cover when they spotted the turtle with the hungry look in its eyes. A goby yelled, "Don't do it! That's my cleaning station! I work there!"

Another pleaded, "I live there!"

Gilgongo laid his face right up against the sweet sponge and rubbed his jowls on it. He looked back at the scared fish. "Just one?" the turtle politely inquired.

A red two-spot cardinal fish approached. "You can't eat just one. Who are you kidding?"

"Listen… I haven't had a sponge for months. I have to have one."

"Not one of these, turtle." The cardinal fish was defiant, but defenseless.

"I'll tell you what," Gilgongo offered, showing his heart was softer than his shell, "you pick the sponge. It doesn't really matter which one to me, so pick the one I'll eat. That's fair."

The fish threw herself in front of a bright yellow branch and proclaimed, "Not this one!"

Another cardinal and several gobies positioned themselves in front of the other sponges and declared their own squatters' rights. Everyone loved having a turtle around when there were jellyfish to be eaten, but nobody wanted one hanging around *their* sponge.

"Hey, I shellpathize, and I'm trying to swim with you here, but I *gotta* eat a sponge. Work with me, please," Gilgongo pleaded.

A goby appeared out of the barrel of a yellow branch. "If you're willing to eat something else, there's a huge loggerhead over the next ridge. It's massive…"

"A loggerhead?! Are you kidding? You think I'd eat my cousin? Why I oughta…" Outraged at the vile suggestion, Gilgongo faced the tiny fish and stuffed his snout into its home while he tried to decide whether to eat the goby, the sponge… or both.

"No, no, no, no, no, not suggesting that you should eat your cousin, no, no, no, nothing like that! Merely pointing out that there's an uninhabited, uneaten, delicious, delectable loggerhead *sponge*, just over the next ridge."

"A loggerhead sponge? Hmm. Is it all covered with sediment and algae?"

"Well, the last time I looked, that was yesterday morning, not much sediment and honestly, a fair amount of algae, but it did…"

Gilgongo was gone. "I love a nice growth of algae with my sponge! Thanks! Sorry about the trouble."

"Don't eat it all," the cardinal fish responded. "We want it to grow back for the next turtle who comes to eat our homes."

The sponge was as large as the goby said. It had a lovely algae icing, not too much sediment. It was perfect, except for one thing. Someone was already eating it. A wisp of silt rose from behind the round mound. Gilgongo was not afraid. Not many vicious predators who could harm the large turtle would be munching sponge, or be able to fit behind it. Still, Gilgongo approached casually, cautiously, but with confidence.

He swung around the back of the grayish purple sponge and saw a well-coifed angelfish munching in a matter of fact fashion. The angel smiled and moved to one side, still eating, but inviting the green turtle to join in.

Gilgongo felt like ripping huge mouthfuls. But, remembering his manners, ate with restraint. As the turtle chewed, he spoke to the fish. "The gobies and the cardinals sent me over here. I almost *manged* their *spange*."

"But you chose not to?"

"Well, even though different sponges do taste differently, uninhabited ones always taste better. No need to be home-nivorous."

"A worthy thought," the angelfish agreed.

"The fish from the yellow tubes asked that I leave enough of this loggerhead that it will grow back. I guess they use it as a substitute when someone wants to taste the tubes."

The angelfish noticed the rebuilt fin. He saw the tag of the man-tide attached to the turtle. "You have just returned, haven't you?"

"I guess it's kinda obvious." Shellfconsciously, Gilgongo tried to tuck the rubber flipper behind and beneath his shell.

"How long were you there?"

"Not as long as the others…"

"Not as long as me."

"You were there too?"

Pagre nodded.

"Maybe we should stop eating," Gilgongo suggested. "Those fish might need to use this sponge sooner rather than later. And there's not much left."

"Eat all you want. The sponge will last."

Gilgongo pulled his face from the feast. An inky dark residue, a spongestash, covered his snout. Pagre also withdrew. He laughed when he saw Gilgongo's face. "Now that's how you should look when you eat a sponge. You should look like you enjoy it."

"Oh, I definitely enjoy it," the turtle said.

"Good, then let's eat some more."

"I don't know. Maybe we should just find another."

"Forgive me. I'm Pagre, and you are?"

"Gilgongo, the name's Gilgongo."

"Well, Gilgongo, what's wrong with this sponge?"

When the turtle looked back at the loggerhead, it was completely re-grown. The turtle nodded his head. "I'm eating with an angel, aren't I?"

"Maybe I'm eating with the angel," Pagre replied. The two returned to the sponge.

"So what were you, an angel, doing in there?"

"Can you think of a better place for me to be? Like you, I was sent."

"Not me, I was dying on a dune when—"

"And now you are alive. We were all sent, selected."

"Well, angel, where are you going now?"

"I'm not sure, but I think I need to stay right here. Seaqoyit isn't done with me or this place just yet. What about you? Where is your mission? Where are you being called?"

"I haven't really thought about it like that, but I seem to be swimming south."

"To the warm water?"

"Yes... that's where I need to go."

"Then go there. Swim with Seaqoyit. Bring him with you."

"Pagre, I'll tell you the truth. I'm a horrible fishtian..."

"Most of us are..."

"...but I feel like the spirit is with me everywhere I go. He shouldn't be. I don't deserve it, but I feel like... even on that dune, even though I was going to die, I never felt alone, hardly even scared."

"You have faith."

"I think I have a friend."

"We all do. And that, Gilgongo, is faith."

The two returned to the never ending sponge. Gilgongo helped himself to huge mouthfuls, swallowed them down and then watched the sponge regenerate, giggling the entire time. He and Pagre chatted and chewed before they parted waves to begin a journey that actually started a long time ago.

The dolphins did not stop swimming until there was no land to be seen anywhere. They paused over a coral patch and rested. It was the first real reef Niv had ever seen. He was speechless as he swam throughout the living mass, searching, investigating. Nhoj was also blown away by the reef. Although he had seen one before, he could not remember it. Soon the two brothers were doing what brothers everywhere do, they played hide and seek, punctuated with a slightly overdone body slam or nip to the fins when one found the other.

Niv saw bubbles rise from behind a wall of sponges and coral. He inched his way forward, trying not to create a swell that would alert Nhoj. Niv came closer. He spotted a tail fluke protruding from behind a giant lavender-tipped anemone. There was nothing quite so satisfying as one-upping your *older* brother. The opportunities appeared so infrequently, that one had to make the most of them. At the moment, Niv owned Nhoj, he was going to shock his brother right into breaching. He opened his mouth and prepared to nip Nhoj…

"Ahh!" It was Niv who was nibbled. He turned and saw his brother beaming behind him.

"You're bit, you're it," Nhoj teased.

Just as Niv was about to body slam his boastful bro, he stopped. "If you just bit me, who belongs to that tail over there?" Niv had always known everyone in the tank. This was really the first time he had encountered a stranger. Was it safe? Perhaps the tail merely belonged to one of his parents. Niv scanned the reef.

Floating in a shaft of sunlight above the youngsters, he could see the silhouette of mom and dad. Turning back to Nhoj, he said, "They're there, we're here, so who's there?"

The concern that flashed across the brother's face, was quickly quaffed to avoid the appearance of alarm. Displaying as much false bravado as he could muster, Nhoj said, "Looks like someone else is down here. Let's see if they want to play."

Following his brother's lead, Niv closed ranks. "Yeah, let's see if they want to play." He punctuated the remark with a snap of his jaws that turned out to be more playful than menacing. In truth, the dolphins were worried. In the tanks everything was really play. In the ocean it was different. Games were a luxury, and often they were played for keeps.

"Okay?" Nhoj asked. "Ready?"

"Ready."

"Right." The dolphins floated in front of the coral wall, staring at the tail behind the anemone.

"Well?" Niv asked.

"Go get 'em," Nhoj replied.

"Me? You go first."

"No, you."

"No, you, you're older."

"I'll cover your flukes," Nhoj proposed.

"I'll cover my own flukes. You go first, scaredy catfish."

"Oh yeah, I'll show who the scaredy catfish is!"

With the two brothers wrestling to decide who would go first, a quiet dolphin finned out from behind the coral cover. Two other youngsters also appeared. They floated, amused by the brotherly chaos, patiently waiting to be noticed. One of them finally clicked, "Hello. Hello?"

The battling brothers paused, Nhoj's front flipper still lodged in Niv's mouth. They were staring at a half dozen dolphins, about the same age and size as themselves.

"Hello," one said as she approached. It was the first female, other than mom, and she didn't count anyway, that they had ever spoken to, although they were so stunned neither brother had actually spoken to her.

She saw the tags. "You must be Onaro's sons. But weren't you taken tides ago?"

"Ah, well, uh…" Nhoj began.

"We, uh… well, we uh, escaped, I guess," Niv added.

"Really?! Escaped the man-tide?!" The dolphins swam closer, several more joining in. "You must tell us all about it," one demanded.

The brothers shared a quick epiphfiny. Could it be possible? Were they shellebrities? They puffed their chests and flexed their flippers. This time around, Nhoj had no qualms about going first. He began, "The sea was angry that day, my friends. Breaking out from the man-tide is no swim in the sun."

"Lemme tell ya," Niv interrupted, "It's not for the faint of fin. No way, dangerous stuff escaping the man-tide."

"That's right, little brother…"

The two dolphins swam off, closely followed by an audience that was completely captivated, but certainly not captive, as it should be.

Janee and Onaro took great joy in their children's interesting account of the escape. It was a moment they had both dreamed of, not sure that it could ever have happened. Janee turned to her mate and asked, "Where are we headed?"

"We're already there," he answered.

"Here? This is the place?"

"This is the place," Onaro smiled.

Norton was gills deep in sand, and loving it. To be part of the ocean again, rooted in its floor with nothing but clear blue above, filled the gazer with glee. He thanked Seaqoyit for sending the wave that released him and prayed that he could survive in this strange new sea so far from home. Norton missed Cariam. It would all be so much better if his friend was with him. The gazer considered whether he'd rather be in the tanks with Cariam alive, or free without his best friend. Norton winced as he remembered how the octopus had answered the question. Cariam trusted in himself and he was gone. Norton had trusted in Seaqoyit, the spirit of the sea, and he was free.

It had been a while since Norton had fed himself the way he was intended to. While it remained to be seen if his timing was off, his senses were still well tuned. The gazer locked in on the meal as it approached. He saw what looked to be a large grouper lumbering his way. Often little fish accompanied larger fish. Sometimes they used them for protection. Other times they used them to steal remnants of meals. Norton watched to see if anything tagged along behind or beneath the fish.

He spotted a speck, translucent and quick, darting below. If he angled himself correctly, Norton could grab the morsel and swim into cover before the grouper gulped the gazer. If it was meant to be, Seaqoyit would deliver the meal. If not, they would pass and Norton would wait for another.

The huge fish passed to the right of Norton. He felt the impressive surge against his face. The fish's shadow veiled the gazer. "It has to be a sign," he thought, "that the meal is mine." A tiny string of sunlight caught the prey and flashed on its flesh, marking it for Norton. The second he saw the sun's spark, Norton lunged from the sand. Even if he missed the mouthful, it felt great to be hunting again. Norton stretched his jaws, burst from below and made off with the meal, throwing himself into a pile of rocks a few fins away.

About to swallow his prey, the gazer was shocked by what happened next. The huge grouper turned and snapped. He pursued Norton into the rocks. "How strange," Norton thought. He had never seen a larger fish take any notice of those vagabonds who swam in its wake. "Perhaps, he thought I was swimming at *him*, but then why wouldn't he just swim off after snapping at me?"

The large fish located Norton easily. It laid its snout next to him, a few rattling rocks separating the two. Norton was shocked again. Perhaps his skills weren't quite as polished as he had believed. The fish was not a grouper at all. Norton didn't know what it was, but it definitely wasn't a grouper. It was massive, with bony scales and terrifyingly twisted teeth. "Let him go," it commanded. "If you swallow my friend, I swallow you."

Maputa could not believe that Shareef would be so careless. She had asked him to tuck himself behind one of her scales just as he did on their journey into captivity, but Shareef wanted to see everything. Whether he put himself in peril or not made no difference. And what happens? The shrimp is swallowed. Now the canth had to interrupt her journey in order to save Shareef. "From here on in, he rides a scale," she whispered to Cariam.

The octopus had a plan as well. While Maputa threatened the offending fish, Cariam released himself, turned sandy brown with white and black flecks, and crawled toward the rocks. Sure that the fish would be consumed by the thought of being consumed, Cariam made use of the diversion. He had seen morays using this same technique while hunting... him. When he arrived at the rocks, he turned a dark gray, with dull streaks of green running across his body. He contracted muscles to change the texture of his flesh so that it mimicked the surface of the rocks.

"Surrender the meal, or become a meal," Maputa continued. "Do it quickly, I'm in a hurry."

Norton was speechless. He was afraid to move. He sat in black shadows behind the rocks and did what gazers do best. He waited. Soon there was another rock next to him. This one was alive.

"I know where you are. I can swallow both you and the rocks. Don't be foolfish, surrender the shrimp," Maputa warned.

Norton decided to comply. He really had no choice. But just

as he was about to speak, Cariam spread his arms and threw himself over the gazer. The octopus enveloped the fish and squeezed. He opened his beak. It was the only hard part of his entire body, but it could cut through a conch.

Norton knew what was coming. After all, his best friend was an octopus. He fired up the electrical pads behind his ears and juiced the octopus with everything he had. The octopus released the gazer. The gazer opened a gill cover so the shrimp could escape. And Maputa, who slammed her face into the disturbance, had her sensitive snout singed by the electricity surging through the water.

When the canth opened her eyes, she saw the octopus back on the gazer, wrapped completely around the fish. With Shareef safely tucked behind a scale, Maputa whispered, "Show's over, let's get going."

"What do you mean? Let's take care of this fish before it zaps Cariam again!" the shrimp protested.

"Stop it, there'll be no more zapping of anyone. That's the friend, what's his name?"

"The gazer? Ah, Newton?"

"Yeah, that's right."

"So what's going on over there? They're not fighting?"

"Nah, Cariam's just hugging his pal."

Maputa turned back to the happy reunion. "Hey, Cariam… Now that you found Newton, are you coming with us or not?"

Cariam released his friend. "I don't know. What do you think, Norton?"

"I don't know. Where are you going?"

Maputa answered, "I'm going home. I have pups and a mate waiting for me."

Shareef stuck his head out and said, "There's no one waiting for me, but I'm going anywave. I'm sticking with 'Puta."

"Well," the canth asked, "anyone else coming along?"

"Can I ask a question, first?" the gazer began. "Do you know where you're going? I mean, I'm sure you do, but do you know how to get *there*... from *here*?"

"Do I know? No. But I'm going to try. Didn't you hear me, I've got a family and a sheaf of canths waiting for me. You're welcome to join us..."

"...or not, Newton," Shareef added.

"You're a coelacanth?" Norton asked rhetorically. "I've never seen a fish like you before, but I've heard that there are brown ones, not as blue as you, living in my sea. And I've been told that your cousins live almost directly west of where Cariam and I are from."

"I have cousins in your sea?"

"I believe you do." The gazer continued, "Right now, we're closer to your home than ours."

"How do you know?" the canth asked hopefully.

"He knows the sky," Cariam explained.

"And if you know the sky, you know the sea..." Norton explained. "It is a long journey, a migration and a half. But I can find the way."

"Then you must come with us!" Maputa declared.

"I think the spirit wants this. We have been brought together, perhaps even as far back as the man-tide's treachery, for a reason. I think Seaqoyit wants us to take you home."

"Then take me home." The canth commanded.

"Cariam, what do you think?" The gazer needed to know if his friend felt the same way.

"We could survive here. This sea will support us nicely, but I think you are right. I think you were right, back in the tank. One way or another, the Spirit's wish will be done. So yes, let's take the journey together. And when it's done, if it's meant to be, we'll be that much closer to Makoona."

"Good," the gazer agreed. "As I said, this is a migration, so we will follow the whale migration routes to start. I will watch the stars."

"I will follow the currents and get us through the deep water," Maputa vowed.

"I will talk to the whales," Cariam promised as he crawled back under the canth and suckered on.

"And I'm not moving from here," Shareef said from behind the large, safe, coelacanth scale. "No way. I learned my lesson. Never leave the canth."

As they set out on their quest for the Indian Ocean, the gazer swam up to Maputa's side and spoke to Shareef. "Hey, sorry about swallowing you before, really. Didn't mean anything by it. And by the wave, since we're gonna be together for a while, the name's actually Norton, not Newton."

"Whatever," the shrimp replied.

"No, really, there's quite a bit of difference. They're two completely different names. I have a friend named Newton. Totally different fish, totally different name."

"Right, whatever," the shrimp went to sleep.

"Well, good. I'm glad we could straighten that out."

"Help! Someone, help me! *Please*, don't go!" a voice screamed from the sand below. Everyone in the group gathered tightly around Maputa and looked down. A minute trace of dust stirred on the flats. They approached slowly.

"Oh, the injustice of it. Don't let them do this to me, not while I'm in my prime! Someone stop the brutes, before it's too late!"

When they saw what was going on, they had to smile. It was horrible, but it was rather funny. A pair of robust two-claw shrimp carried a comet starfish back to their home under a rocky plateau. They had the star turned upside down so that it could not use its suction tipped podia to grab onto anything. With its undersurface exposed, the ex-fins from SeaTopia could hear every word the startled star screamed.

For the most part, fish ate and fish were eaten. There usually wasn't much discussion about it. You used whatever abilities

Seaqoyit gave you, but everyone pretty much kept quiet whether they were predator or prey. That's just the wave it was. This starfish, however, was making quite a fuss.

"I'm on it," Shareef said, slipping out from the canth's protective scale, ignoring his previous proclamation that still echoed in a swirling swell behind him.

"Wait up," the octopus called, "what do you think you're doing?"

"Don't worry, I'm a crustacean. These are my shrimps." Shareef landed on a piece of water-logged wood and called to the two-claws, "What up, reefy?"

"Eating," one answered. "You've heard of that?"

"Don't try and take her," the other added, "this is our meal."

"Meal! Oh, Spirit no! Friend, confidant, advisor, mentor; yes… but *meal.* No! Not me! I have so much more to offer."

"Why don't you just eat her right here, right now?" Shareef asked.

"Not much of a shrimp, are ya? If we ever get her home and can keep her turned over, we can eat this starfish for ten tides, easy."

"I don't know if I could listen to her for ten tides," Shareef quipped.

"You got a point there," the other shrimp agreed.

"Nah, there's so much food here. We'll just ignore her."

"This is not how it's supposed to be," the comet whined. "There's so much more that I have to do with my life. I finally escape the man-tide and now I'm going to die! *Eaten alive!* Oh why, Seaqoyit? Why *me?"*

Shareef's tentacles snapped to attention. He pointed his eye stalks at the starfish and carefully looked her over. Five arms, one a touch shorter than the others, still growing back. A healthy orange-brown color. There it was. A tiny blue bead attached at the base of her central disk. She was in the tanks. Shareef shot back to the rest of the group.

"So what's going on?" Cariam asked.

"The starfish has received an invitation to dinner with the shrimp."

"Okay, so let's go," Maputa demanded.

"Well, there's a—for want of a better term—catch. The starfish, she's one of us."

"What does that mean?" Norton asked.

"It means, she was in the tanks, like us. And she just escaped, like us."

"But she's about to be eaten," Cariam continued, "not like us. Let's go."

Maputa nodded.

"What are you thinking?" Norton asked Shareef.

"I'm usually not the sentimental type, but imagine being where we were, getting out and before you can have lunch, you are lunch. Let's get her out of there."

The octopus scratched his mantle. "It's not our business. We can't take her unless we're gonna eat her."

"Or unless the shrimp give her to us," Shareef added.

"Why would they do that?" Maputa asked. "Besides, we're wasting time. Let's go."

"With what's facing us, a little time now won't matter... She was in the tanks. Let's see what Shareef can do," Norton suggested.

Without waiting for any further approval, Shareef swam off. "I'll be right back," he called.

The two-claws were making very slow progress. Shareef landed on the same log as his previous visit and said, "Shrimp, is she a screamer. If it were me, I'd dump her. There's got to be other stuff to eat."

"Yes, great idea!" the comet cooed. "Dump her. I mean, dump me. I'm not very tasty, you know."

"Nah, we came this far, might as well get something out of it."

"Dump me. Dump me. Dump me. Dump me. Dump me."

"Will you shut up!? You're making me crazy!"

The other shrimp tweaked the star with a pincer.

"*Ahh!* Torture? What kind of shrimp are you?! Oh, the infishanity of it. Why did I ever leave the tanks?! What was I thinking?!"

"Shut up!" The shrimp turned to his partner. "I tell ya, she's driving me crazy."

"Don't worry, after a tide or two she'll be quiet."

Shareef grinned. "Why don't you give her to me?"

"Give? Then we would have nothing to show for all our trouble. I have no intention of being left empty-clawed."

That gave Shareef an idea. "How about this?" he proposed. "You can have a piece of her. Take an arm for your trouble. It makes no sound. It's easy to carry. And you'll have a nice meal."

"An *arm?* You're giving pieces of me away?!!"

"Shh," Shareef soothed.

"So he gets an arm? What's that do for me?" asked the other shrimp.

"I'm sure your pal will share it."

"Not a chance. My arm," he said.

"So what about me?"

Shareef thought for a second. "You take one, too."

"'*You take one, too.*' I'm still here, you know. I can hear you!"

"Yeah, she's got five…"

"Well, really four and a half… And I don't want the small one!"

"Me either…"

"Don't worry," Shareef interrupted, "everyone gets a full arm, plenty to go around."

The comet star looked like she was about to faint, but she didn't.

"Okay, we each get an arm, you get the rest of her, mouth

included, and it's a done deal."

"How do we get the arms?"

They all looked at the starfish. "They don't just fall off!" she yelled.

"That answers that question." Shareef waved a pincer at Maputa. She and the others swam down to the log. "Cariam, slap a sucker on this mouthy comet and stick two arms in Maputa's mouth. When I click my claw, take 'em both off at the base, okay?"

The canth concurred, "No problem."

"But don't swallow them. They're for these two." Shareef pointed to the two-claws, who smiled and waved.

The starfish was screaming about pain and suffering and whatever else came to her mind. She was in mid-sentence, something like, "This is why they call it *star*vation," when Shareef clicked his claw.

SNAP.

The two arms floated down to the shrimps. They picked them up and left without words. The starfish, however, had words.

"What am I gonna do with two and a half arms? I'll never survive—"

"Stop it," Cariam said. "I've lost an arm before and done just fine."

"You've got *seven* more. I got two and a half!"

"No, Cariam's right," Norton said. "Stop it. Look at what you have, not what you don't have. Make the best of it. In fact, you should be thanking us. Stop complaining. Hey, I know you. You were in the reef tank. But I didn't know you could speak. You didn't say a word back there."

"Well, I wasn't being dragged off to be eaten alive back there!"

"And no one's dragging you off now either," Shareef pointed out. It was his polite way of saying, "shut up."

"Okay, let's get swimming," Maputa urged. "Our work here

is done." Shareef and Cariam climbed aboard. The octopus draped himself in front of the canth's dorsal fin, just behind her head.

"What about me?" the starfish asked.

"What about you?" Cariam answered.

"Take me, too."

"You have no idea where we're going," Maputa said.

"I know exactly where you're going. You are going to the caves of the canths. And you," the starfish pointed to the gazer and the octopus, "are going to Makoona."

Everyone in the group froze. They looked at Shareef. "I didn't tell her anything!"

"How do you know what you know?" Norton asked.

Now, when everyone wanted her to speak, the comet was quiet. Norton repeated his question.

"You may read the stars, gazer, but I speak to them," the starfish claimed. "Let me come with you. I can help."

The group reached consensus without discussion. It seemed as though it was meant to be. Cariam picked up the starfish. She attached herself to Maputa's gill cover. She whispered, "Seaqoyit's stars look down upon everything. There is a lot they can tell us."

The group of four had become five. They were united by a single purpose, a single journey, a single planet, a single Spirit. And so, the five actually became one. They would need to be, because now they really were out there, somewhere.

About the Author

John Morano is a professor of journalism at Monmouth University in New Jersey. He also served as the founding Editor-in-Chief of ROCKbeat Magazine, Managing Editor of Modern Screen Magazine and Senior Editor for Inside Books Magazine.

A writer very concerned with endangered species and habitat depletion, he has spent most of his life living on or near the ocean and enjoys using the sea as a primary setting. His other books in the *Eco-Adventure* series include *Makoona* and *A Wing and a Prayer*.

Morano's formal education includes the institutions of Penn State University, Clark University and Adelphi University.

Bonus Features

It's not your favorite premium DVD. It's a Blue Works novel for young adults. We pack every Blue Works novel with "extras" because our books are created at premium quality — no mass-production, no newspaper print pages, no formula stories. With every purchase of a Blue Works novel you'll receive some or all of these incredible features:

Downloadable from our webcenter:

- A full-color locker poster.
- An extensive study guide written by the author.
- A "Making Of" interview with the author and others.
- Deleted or extra scenes.
- Fan-fiction links where readers take the story further.

By sending us your receipt:

- A limited edition book cover trading card, with statistics.
- A full-color bookmark.
- An autographed Blue Card™. This archival-quality, deep blue, luminescent, mica-speckled card is hand-signed by the author.

So visit us today at
www.windstormcreative.com/blueworks

Or send us a copy of your receipt at
Blue Works
c/o Windstorm Creative
Post Office Box 28
Port Orchard WA 98366

For a partial listing of other great Blue Works novels, turn the page.

Blue Works YA Novels

Take 20% off every book at our webcenter. And while you're there, use eTalk™ to ask your favorite author a question, download or request the first chapter of any book, and much more.

FICTION
And Featuring Bailey Wellcom as the Biscuit (Peggy Durbin)
Awakening Curry Buckle (Michael Donnelly)
The Brute (Mike Klaassen)
Makoona (John Morano)
Mrs. Estronsky and the UFO (Pat Schmatz)
The Pirate Queen (Christina Bauer)
Present from the Past (Janet & Mike Golio)
Puzzle from the Past (Janet & Mike Golio)
A Wing and a Prayer (John Morano)

SCIENCE FICTION & FANASTY
2176: Birth of the Belt Republic (Ted Butler)
The Legend of Zamiel Zimbalist:
Book Two in the Connedim (Pamela Keyes)
Menace Beyond the Moon (Ted Butler)
Missionary Kids # 1: Journey to Mars (Bobbie Benton Hull)
Missionary Kids # 2: Mars Base Alpha One
(Bobbie Benton Hull)
The Mythfits (Gary Goldstein)
On a Distant World (Joseph Yenkavitch)
Merlin's Door: Book One, Outside of Time series
(Wim Coleman & Pat Perrin)
The Rune of Zachary Zimbalist:
Book One in the Connedim (Pamela Keyes)